By Cassia Leo
http://cassialeo.com

UNMASKED

Volume Two

by Cassia Leo

First Edition

Cover art by Sarah Hansen at Okay Creations.

ISBN-13: 978-1499608229

ISBN-10: 1499608225

CONTENTS

CHAPTER ONE

Out of the darkness and into the light, a new Alex Carmichael is reborn.

I repeat this mantra in my head as I enter my new home. Drawing in deep breaths, I attempt to sooth myself after a stressful trip to the market, in broad daylight. A few minutes of this, then I head for the kitchen.

The kitchen in this one-hundred-fourteen-year-old cottage has an odd smell, like wet cement. It could be the crumbling plaster on the walls, or the slightly damp wood floors, which never seem to dry due to the humidity.

I open a tiny cupboard above the sink and put

away my six new drinking glasses, purchased at a shop a few blocks away, which sells cheap housewares. Six drinking glasses for €1,49 and six dinner plates for €2,00. My first day on this tiny island in the middle of the Atlantic Ocean, I was a little confused by the comma in the place of the decimal point and the exchange rate. But three days in, I can do the math in my head now.

I put away the plates in the same cupboard, then I open the refrigerator to put away the fruits and vegetables I got at the open-air market just around the corner. I try not to think about the incident with the prickly pear from my last day in Los Angeles. But I also can't let myself forget. I need to remember that, however slim, there is a possibility that Daimon is still alive. It's possible I was so distraught that I missed a faint pulse in his neck. I must remember this so I can be ready for him.

I grab an apple out of the brown paper bag and just as I set it down on the shelf in the fridge, a knock at the door startles me. Slowly, I close the refrigerator door and lift the back of my shirt to slide my knife out of its holster. Stepping into the tiny living room, I glance at the two windows on each side of the front door, but I can't see anyone. My heart races as I step closer. Finally, I slowly push aside the cover on the peephole and peer through.

I let out a deep sigh. It looks like a neighbor here to welcome me with a bottle of wine. I want to pretend I'm not home, but I can't. I left my mask behind in L.A. No more hiding.

I slip the knife back into its holster and open the door. The man standing before me looks somewhat familiar. I think I may have seen him cutting some branches on a tree just down the lane.

"*Hola! Mucho gusto. Bienvenido a La Palma. Soy tu nuevo vecino,* Nicolas."

I stare into his shiny green eyes for a moment, trying to remember one of the few Spanish phrases I have memorized, but I'm dumbfounded. "*No habla español.* I'm Alyssa."

I don't speak Spanish. I'm Alyssa.

I chose the name Alyssa because it sounds close enough to Alex that I think it will be easy for me to get used to. And it sounds innocent. I need people to think I'm innocent. Because I *was* innocent, until I invited Daimon into my apartment.

"You must be American," he replies, his lips curling into a charming grin.

His eyes crinkle at the edges when he smiles and his skin is golden and tanned. He must work in the sun and he must be at least thirty years old. I don't even know how old Daimon was. *Is?*

"Yes, I'm American. I'm here on holiday."

"Oh, what a shame you're only here temporarily. Are you leaving soon?" He tucks the bottle of wine behind his back, as if my response will determine whether or not I'm worthy of a welcome gift.

"No, I actually don't know when I'm leaving. Could be a week or a month. Maybe longer. I'm … a photographer. I go wherever inspiration calls."

Though I've already taken the time to set up my new persona by purchasing an expensive camera and photography supplies, saying the words *I'm a photographer* aloud feels strange. The whole purpose of leaving the States was so that I could take off my mask. Finally be myself. And, in essence, I'll be hiding in plain sight. The artist disguise feels at odds with this philosophy.

"A photographer." He raises his eyebrows as he repeats these words, then he pulls the bottle out from behind his back. "I brought you a welcome gift. It's from my cousin's vineyard. I got in last night and there were four cases waiting for me."

The skeptic in me wonders if this guy works for Daimon and he's trying to poison me. The safe thing would be to take the bottle of wine and thank him. Then flush it down the sink the moment he's gone. But when do I ever play it safe?

At that moment, a black man in a dark hoodie passes by and waves at me. Why is everyone here so damn friendly?

I wave back at the man, then I take the bottle from my new neighbor's hand and flash him my best half-albino smile. "Thank you very much.

Would you like to come inside and enjoy a glass?"

He grins at me for a moment in silence. He wasn't expecting an invitation so soon.

"I would love to."

I open the steel storm door wide and he gives me a gentlemanly nod as he passes over the threshold. There should be a similar test for traitors as there is for vampires. Like, if you feed them garlic, they're forced to tell the truth. Or if you splash them with holy water, they instantly give up the name of the person they're working for.

Oh, Alex. You really should stop watching so much TV.

My father's voice is clear in my head. The memory makes my chest tighten with a rush of anger. I set the bottle of wine on top of the tiny, square kitchen table and head for the cupboard where I just put away the drinking glasses.

"Please have a seat," I say, reaching into the cupboard. "Oh, shoot!"

"What's wrong?"

I turn around and he's halfway between

standing and sitting in a chair at the table.

I smile at the awkwardness of his pose. "I forgot to buy a corkscrew when I went to the store today."

He chuckles as he stands up and grabs the bottle of wine off the table. "That's okay. I can open it without a corkscrew. Do you have a sharp knife?"

He takes the two long strides it takes until he's almost face to face with me. I stare at the bottle of wine in his hand until I remember I have to be confident. Looking up into his eyes, I'm caught off guard by the inquisitive look on his face. One eyebrow cocked, self-assured smile, just waiting for me to produce a sharp knife. Probably so he can stab me in the heart.

I let out a coquettish giggle. "Of course I have a knife."

My hand disappears behind me and whips out my knife in a flash. He scrunches his eyebrows together, dissatisfied with this display.

"You carry a knife on you?"

"Single woman in a new town."

His Adam's apple bobs as he swallows hard, then he slowly reaches for my knife. I smile as he gently slips the handle out of my grip and turns toward the sink. He holds the top of the bottle over the basin and, in one swift motion, he chops off the top two inches from the neck of the bottle. A good third of a cup of red wine spills out and into the sink, but he rights the bottle before anymore is lost.

I step forward and peer into the sink at the few chunks of glass and red liquid splattered over the porcelain and can't help but feel impressed. "Quite crafty, aren't you…?"

"Nicolas," he reminds me. "But you may call me Nick."

And how could I forget? Nicolas with the perfectly bronze skin and shiny green eyes. And the fascinating knife skills. *I'll have to keep an eye on you, Nick.*

He smiles then reaches for a towel on the counter. "I'll clean it up."

I try to take the towel from his hand, but he

doesn't let go. "You don't have to do that. I'll clean it up." His smile softens as he lets go of the cloth. "You can pour the wine."

He reaches around me and grabs the drinking glasses, then he grabs the bottle and takes them both to the table. I mop up shards of glass and wine with the dish towel and toss them all, towel included, into the garbage bin beneath the sink. I wash my hands and take a seat across the table from Nick.

He slides my glass of wine across the table. "To new places," he says, raising his in the air, "good lighting," —he winks—"and new friends. *Salud!*"

We clink glasses and I bring mine to my lips slowly, waiting for him to take the first sip. Then it dawns on me that it doesn't matter if he drinks that whole glass. Since I was too busy cleaning up the mess in the sink, I didn't watch him pour my wine. I can't drink this.

I set the glass down gently on the table as he takes a couple of gulps.

"You don't drink wine?" he asks.

I shake my head. "I've never actually drunk alcohol before and my father told me never to accept a drink from a stranger unless they too are willing to drink from the same glass."

I feel a twist of regret in my stomach for bringing my father into this.

"Your father sounds like a smart man." He reaches for my glass of wine and downs the whole thing in a few gulps, then he sets it down on the table looking very satisfied with himself. "See. No poison."

I smile as I reach for the half-empty bottle and pour us both another glass. I have to blend in. I have to immerse myself in the island culture. Drinking a glass or two of wine per day is supposed to be good for you.

Still, I wait for him to take the first sip, then I take mine. The wine is acidic and musky with a sweet berry finish. I like it.

"So what kind of things do you photograph? Nature, architecture, people…?" he asks.

Though his Spanish accent is very noticeable,

he speaks English quite well. And his voice is smooth and crisp. I can understand every word he says.

I take another sip as I contemplate his question, then I flash him a girly smile. "People."

As expected, this response makes him feel comfortable enough to allow his gaze to linger on my albino left eye and the white patch of skin that covers most of the left side of my face. A photographer who looks like me would be expected to shun people. And the old Alex most certainly did. But Alyssa is different. She embraces her flaws.

It makes you different. Different is good. Daimon's voice is still so clear in my mind. His words so soothing. How is it that the man who killed my father, the man I killed just four days ago, still has the power to fill me with such warmth and longing? The very thought of him should send me into a tirade. He deceived me! He used me and my body and he didn't even have the guts to confess he murdered my father.

He also didn't have the courage to kill me.

Or so he claimed. I don't know what to believe anymore. But that's why I'm here on this island. I'm going to find out if anything Daimon said to me the night of the masquerade ball was true.

I drain the rest of the wine from my glass and set it down. "I photograph anything, but mostly people. I do portraits. Would you like your portrait taken?"

His gaze continues to roam over my face, then he smiles. "I would like that."

"Excellent." I fan my face as I suddenly feel flushed. "What do you do for a living?"

"I make sunglasses." I let out a soft chuckle and he shakes his head in dismay. "I know. It's not as glamorous as being a beautiful photographer who travels the world, but it pays well."

"And you're here on vacation?"

"Yes. I don't know for how long. I'm staying in my Great-Aunt Marta's house. She passed away eight years ago, so the house has been empty. I'm going to relax for a little while. Restore the house and maybe the garden. I'm … I'm trying to, as they say, find myself."

"At your age?" I clap my hand over my mouth and he laughs.

"I'm only thirty-two. How old are you?"

"Twenty-one."

Most women lie to make themselves younger. This whole situation with Daimon aged me two years in the span of four days. I knew he was bad for me.

Bad in all the right ways? asks a sexy French voice in my head.

No!

Oh, God. I'm going nuts.

Nick stands up suddenly and this snaps me out of my Daimon-haze. "Are you leaving?"

"Yes. It's almost sundown and I still have a water heater to install. Or I won't be able to shower tomorrow."

I stand up and follow him toward the door. "That would be unfortunate."

"For who?" he asks quickly and I hesitate. He laughs as he reaches for the doorknob. "I'm kidding, Alyssa. It was very nice meeting you. I'm sure you'll be seeing me very soon for that portrait. Shall I bring my Heart of the Ocean necklace?"

I grab the edge of the door as he steps outside and does a half-turn so I can see him from the side with the sun setting behind him. He has a great ass.

"Alyssa?"

My gaze snaps up, away from his ass to his face, and he's grinning. "Yes, sure. That would be great. See you later."

I close the door and lean up against it, savoring the way the cool steel feels against my skin through the thin fabric of my T-shirt. I'm flustered by his good looks and sense of humor. He's so congenial. But, still, all I can think of right now is Daimon.

What would he think of me having a drink with another man? He would not like it one bit. I guess it's a good thing he's dead.

CHAPTER TWO

His body is so solid. That's all I can think as my fingers bump along his ab muscles and down to his thick erection. I wrap my fingers around him and he smiles as the shower water cascades over his glistening muscles.

"Grip it firmly, *chérie*."

I tighten my grip on his solid girth and slowly slide my hand down the velvety length. Stepping forward, I press the tip against my clit, then I plunge my hips forward so his cock glides between my lips. I moan and he wraps his arm around the small of my back to hold me still. I tilt my head back and he sucks hard on the column of my throat. That's going to leave a mark.

Rocking his hips slowly back and forth, he rubs his erection against my clit, using my moisture to guide him in and out of my swollen flesh. His hands grip my ass, then his left hand pulls my leg up, resting my ankle on his shoulder. He slides into my pussy easily, but he's so hard it sends a shock of pain through me.

"Ow."

"Does it hurt?" he asks, as he stretches me.

"Yes."

"Good."

He grips my ass and pushes himself deeper inside me. I yelp in pain and he runs his tongue along the crease of my mouth.

"Scream for me, Alex."

He pushes me up against the wall of the shower and his pelvic bone grinds into my clit as I cry out in pain and ecstasy. "Daimon!"

"Louder," he growls, sinking his teeth into my neck.

"Daimon!"

"I'm going to *destroy* you."

He licks the tender skin on my neck where he just bit me, tracing his tongue all the way up to my jawline then to my lips. He takes my top lip into his mouth and sucks hard as he grinds against my clit. The pulling and the grinding is driving me insane.

"Oh, please, Daimon. Don't stop."

He curls his hips further, digging deeper inside me, crushing my swollen bud with the force of each thrust. The one leg I'm standing on begins to weaken and I coil my arms tightly around his neck for support.

"I want you to come when I come."

"I'm going to come now," I breathe a warning, but he doesn't slow down. My leg trembles and my stomach muscles begin to clench. "I'm coming!"

"Not until I say so!"

"I'm coming! I can't stop! Oh, God!"

He grabs a chunk of hair on the back of my head and thrusts his tongue into my mouth as he pounds my pussy. I release guttural, high-pitched screams as he continues to drive into my sensitive clit. Then he groans into my mouth as he comes inside me.

He continues to kiss me, tenderly, as his hips move oh-so-slowly back and forth. Until his throbbing cock finally softens inside me and I let out a deep sigh.

"I love you, Alex."

The words take me by surprise, so much so that I open my eyes and my stomach clenches at the sight before me. I'm in the tiny bedroom of my rental cottage in La Palma. The morning sunlight is streaming through the sheer curtains. The blankets and sheets are pushed off the bed and into a pile on the wooden floor. My nightgown is pulled up to my neck and the black panties I wore to sleep are missing.

Instinctively, I reach down to cover myself up and find my pussy is soaking wet and my clit is sensitive, as if it's been overstimulated. Was I touching myself in my sleep? I've never done that before.

Something smells … *different* in here. The hairs on my arms stand on end as I inhale the scent of something briny. Images of my dream flash in my mind and I quickly yank down my nightgown to cover myself up. A wave of shame rolls through me as I slide off the bed to retrieve the covers. I toss them haphazardly onto the mattress and head straight for the shower to wash away my embarrassment.

How can I have such poisonous dreams of

Daimon after what he did to me?

The body knows only what the body wants. It doesn't care about the consequences to the mind or the heart.

I push back the pink shower curtain and reach my hand in to turn the water on. Peeling off my nightgown, I toss it into the pedestal sink basin and look at myself in the mirror. I force myself to stare directly at the white streak of hair on the left side of my head and the white blotches of skin on the same side of my face. I used to avoid mirrors at all costs, but everything changed the night I met Detective Daimon Rousseau.

He didn't just change me into a woman. He changed me into a woman with a purpose. And my purpose was to make him pay for what he did to my father.

Out of the darkness and into the light, a new Alex was reborn as Alyssa.

I trace my fingertips down my left cheek, over my neck and down to my breast. My nipples are a bit darker. Maybe I was rubbing or pinching them in my sleep. That was quite a dream I had of Daimon.

I resist the urge to move my hand further down

and touch myself to the memory of my dream. Instead, I step inside the shower and force myself to sing, loudly, so I don't have to think of Daimon and his beautiful cock.

Oh, get a hold of yourself, Alex, I reprimand myself silently.

I take a quick shower, running the water a bit colder than normal to cool my hot, aching skin. Then I hurry into a pair of jeans, white tank top, and sandals. Looking at myself in the mirror, I realize the jeans look far too much like the old Alex. I change into a soft turquoise jersey skirt and sigh with a bit of relief. My legs are so white from not wearing anything but jeans for the past nine months. You can hardly see the white patches of skin on my left leg.

I grab a canvas grocery bag from the hook inside the tiny walk-in pantry. Then I hang my camera around my neck and make my way outside. Closing the front door behind me, I turn around to face the Atlantic Ocean. It looks just like a "wish you were here" greeting card. Picture perfect.

And the smells.... The whole island smells briny and sun-baked. Mix in some of the local aromas of tropical flowers, the savory smells from people cooking in their homes, and the sweet, earthy smell of grapevines. I could get used to this kind of life.

But I mustn't get *too* comfortable. I have to appear comfortable on the outside. Inside, I have to remain self-conscious and vigilant.

I set off down the lane toward the open-air market with one thought in mind: *Out of the darkness and into the light.* I have to blend in with everyone else here, and they're all so damn *happy.*

A squat woman with brown wrinkled skin, wearing a flowery apron over her gauzy dress, smiles at me from where she's sweeping her front stoop. Her husband sits in a chair at the far end of their porch, his bottom lip jutting out farther as if he's lost his top teeth. He waves at me then flashes me a partially-toothless grin.

I smile and wave at both of them. "*Hola!*"

They must be silently wondering who this strange looking girl is who just moved in next door. I'll introduce myself to them soon, when I have a bit more time. Today, I have to get to the market before all the *ensaimadas* are gone. *Ensaimadas* are decadently soft bread rolls filled with sweet pastry cream and dusted with powdered sugar. I've only had one since arriving in La Palma, but I've already deciphered that they are quite popular here as a breakfast item. If I don't get to the market soon, they'll run out.

At the crossing, I turn the corner and I can smell the market from a block away. It always smells like a combination of fresh fish, fruit, and baked goods. A young kid, maybe mid- to late-teens is standing next to a bicycle outside a convenience store. He stares at my white hair so unabashedly, I'm afraid he's going to drop the bike at any moment. I force a smile and he flashes me a weak smile in return.

I really should be used to this by now. This is what I've been dealing with since the moment I left my apartment four days ago. From the moment I stepped into the taxi that drove me to the airport and the cab driver did a double-take when he saw two different colored eyes, my stomach has been clenched tight as a fist.

I'm trying really hard not to get angry with people for expressing their natural shock and curiosity. After all, millions of years of evolution has taught us to shun undesirable mutations. There's no use in arguing with a person's natural instincts. But it still hurts.

I arrive at the bakery stand where a long folding table is covered in an orange and blue striped tablecloth. Half the pastries are already gone, gobbled up by the early risers, but there are still three *ensaimadas* left. I point at them then hold up two fingers.

"*Uno cincuenta,*" the merchant woman says as she begins to put them in a white paper bag.

I don't know what this means, but I know *uno* means one, so I give her two euros. She hands me back fifty cents. So *cincuenta* must mean fifty. I'll have to remember that.

I smile and say thank you in Spanish, then I use hand motions to ask if I can take her picture. She smiles for the camera and I say *gracias* a few times before I head back toward Dolores Street, the narrow lane I live on. Also the narrow lane that my new friend Nick lives on, which is where I'm headed. A dark flitter of movement in my peripheral vision catches my attention as I pass the convenience store, but when I turn toward it there's nothing there. My eyes flit back and forth at both sides of the street, glancing over both shoulders then forward again. Nothing and no one but locals here.

It's hard to let go of that paranoid sense of being watched. My father had been watching me every night for eight months. I'd grown so accustomed to that feeling. It made me both uneasy and comfortable at once knowing he was keeping an eye on me. I didn't know I was also being watched for months by Daimon. It's only natural I'm still on edge.

I turn left onto Dolores and the gravity of the downhill slope is urging me toward the tiny gray stucco cottage on the right side of the lane. The house is set back from the iron gate surrounding the property and the grass is a bit overgrown, but he did mention that he's only been here a day or so. I'm sure he'll be outside pushing a lawnmower with no shirt on very soon.

I lift the latch on the waist-high gate and slide it aside. Pushing it open, I step onto the cracked concrete pathway leading toward the small cottage. I close the gate softly behind me and make my way toward the front door.

Something about the fact that he's not up at nine o'clock in the morning, already working on taming this unruly garden, disconcerts me. I can't help but think of Daimon. By nine o'clock, Daimon would have this garden tamed with at least three adversaries buried beneath the soil.

I knock on the dark wood door with the intricate carvings and wait. My heart pounds as I realize I didn't prepare a greeting in my head. What am I going to say? *Hi, I brought you some bread!* Not very clever or sexy, but—

The door opens, interrupting my thoughts as I'm rendered speechless. Nick is standing before me in nothing but black boxer briefs. His hand is rubbing his face, attempting to wipe away the cobwebs of sleep clinging to his drowsy expression. His bare chest is smooth and golden with a light patch of hair trailing from his navel and downward, disappearing underneath the waistband of his boxers. Right above that bulge. I have a strong urge to photograph him right now.

"Alyssa?"

I snap my eyes upward and he looks stupefied by my presence. "I'm sorry. I didn't mean to wake you. I just… I brought you something… to thank you for the bottle of wine."

Don't look at the bulge. Don't look at the bulge.

He glances at the white paper bag in my hand

and smiles. "You didn't have to do that. What is it?"

"Um ..." I look down at the bag and catch another glimpse of his boxers, then quickly look up. "Bread?"

"Bread?" I nod and he chuckles as he opens the door wider. "Come inside and we can share this bread."

I step over the threshold and into his living room. It's small but more modern than I would have expected considering he's only been here for a couple of days and it used to belong to his great-aunt. The white sofa and heavy wood coffee table are anchored by a soft gray area rug. Beneath the rug are light beechwood floors that extend into an open dining area and kitchen.

"Have a seat at the table. I'm going to put on some clothes."

I smile as he heads toward the hallway on the left and I head for the dining table. Passing a small black desk set against the wall, I can't help but notice a passport and two photo identification cards lying on the surface. I pause, tempted to pick them up to see what kind of IDs they are, but the sound of footsteps stops me.

I turn around and his eyebrow is cocked as he approaches. He brushes past me and opens the top drawer of the desk. Then he sweeps all the IDs into the drawer and quickly slides it closed.

He smiles as he gently places his hand on the small of my back. "Come. Sit. I'll make some coffee."

I take a seat at a dark wood dining table in the kitchen, but I don't bother telling him that I don't drink the stuff. I might as well give it a try. I tried the wine last night and it wasn't so bad. But I'll have to watch him carefully while he prepares it.

He's wearing a blue T-shirt that clings a little to his chest and shoulder muscles. The jeans he wears look perfectly distressed, just like his dark hair. From a shelf above the steel kitchen counter, he grabs a glass French press coffee maker and he begins spooning some coffee into it from a jar. He seems very at ease and this house feels very lived in. It doesn't seem like it was empty for years.

He carries the French press and two mugs to the table and sets them down in front of me. "Do you take your coffee with milk and sugar?"

"Yes. Thank you."

I keep my eye on him as he retrieves a small

carton of milk from the stainless steel refrigerator and a small jar from the counter. Grabbing a couple of spoons from a drawer, he sits across from me at the table and pours me a cup. I don't know the first thing about how much milk and sugar goes into a cup of coffee, so I take a guess and put a splash of milk and three spoons of sugar. When I taste it, it's very sweet, but I don't say this.

"Very good."

He pours himself a cup, but he doesn't add any milk or sugar. He quietly sips from his mug for a minute or two while watching me. Then his face gets very serious.

"Forgive me, but I have to ask about this."

He reaches forward and I flinch a little when he gently grabs a piece of my white streak of hair. I push his hand away and take a deep breath as I remind myself not to retreat inward. It's a simple question.

"I'm a chimera. I have two sets of DNA." He scrunches his eyebrows together in confusion and I sigh. "This is why I'm here. I've been hiding all of my life. I just wanted to go somewhere I could be myself."

My stomach hurts at the painful truth buried in

this lie.

He smiles and tilts his head. "It's quite beautiful. You look like a superhero." I laugh and he smiles even wider as he leans forward. "You also have a beautiful laugh."

Flattery. He wants something.

I reach for the white bag and push it across the table so it's between us. "Aren't you going to eat?"

He reaches into the bag and pulls out an *ensaimada.* Then he takes a huge bite, getting powdered sugar all over his lips and a bit on the tip of his nose.

"These are my favorite," he says through a mouthful of bread. "How did you know?"

I smile at his goofiness as a strange warmth grows inside my belly. But I can't help but feel as if something is off. I don't know how to talk to him. He's not like Daimon. He's not like me. He's normal.

"I should get going."

I rise from the table and he tosses his bread back into the bag. "I'll walk you home."

I chuckle and immediately wonder if I'm doing it just because he complimented my laugh. "That's not necessary," I say when I reach the front door.

"I'm just two houses down on the other side of the street."

"I know. You're closer to the ocean than I am. I'm jealous." He stands with his hand on the door handle, making no attempt to open the door so I can leave. "Would you like to come with me to a dinner party tomorrow night? A friend of the family would like to welcome me to the island. Any excuse to get drunk."

"Yes," I reply before I can overthink my way out of it.

"Beautiful!"

I'm tempted to reach up and wipe away the powdered sugar on his nose. Instead, I tap the tip of my nose and smile. "You have some sugar on your nose. And a little right there on your lip, too."

He squints at me. "I put it there for you."

"What?"

Without warning, he leans forward and plants a soft kiss on my lips. I can smell the coffee and sugar on his breath as his mouth hovers over mine, waiting for me to respond. My heart is pounding so hard it hurts. Daimon's voice sounds in my mind: *When you scream, you scream my name. When you come, you come for me. When you dream, you dream of me.*

I reach up and clasp my hand around the back of Nick's solid neck to pull his lips hard against mine. I need to exorcise Daimon and his haunting voice from my mind.

His lips taste sugary and his tongue is a bit bitter from the coffee. I can only compare him to Daimon, so I must admit to myself that he doesn't kiss better than Daimon did. But that's probably because he is the one who taught me how to kiss, so naturally I'm going to believe his way is the right way. Didn't Daimon also teach me that different is good? Nick doesn't kiss bad. Just different.

A loud bang startles us both and we quickly turn toward the sound. The outside of the window overlooking the front garden is streaked with something dark.

"What was that?"

He shakes his head. "I don't know."

He opens the door and I follow him outside to the front yard. We step off the concrete path into the overgrown grass. He squats down in front of the window and sweeps aside a tangle of weeds to expose a dead crow lying on the dry earth.

"It must have flown into the window," he says, standing up. "Maybe I shouldn't keep the windows so clean."

"Or maybe he saw us kissing and he got jealous."

He laughs but, as soon as I speak these words aloud, I realize this may not be too far from the truth.

CHAPTER THREE

Nick arrives at my cottage to take me to the dinner party just after eight in the evening. One thing I really like about this island is that everyone eats dinner late at night. It's not uncommon to see the lights on and a family sitting at the table for dinner at ten or eleven p.m. Sometimes later. Though I'm trying to break my habit of existing only in the darkness, I can't deny the comfort it brings me. The darkness is like my security blanket and, after nineteen years of clinging to it, it's very difficult to let it go.

I step outside, not bothering to lock the door.

This is not Los Angles. No one here locks their front door.

Turning around to face Nick, I'm not surprised to see him eyeballing my dress. I got the dress last night at a tiny boutique near the housewares store. It's not a high-end boutique. The dresses were displayed just a few feet away from a rack of football (soccer) jerseys. But it's white and gauzy with skinny spaghetti straps, which will allow me to tan.

A tan will make my white skin discolorations more pronounced, but that's okay. I'm not just going to accept my condition. I'm going to flaunt it.

Fake it till you make it, right?

"You look like a Greek goddess," Nick remarks, extending his arm for me to latch on.

I smile, but I don't lock my arm in his. "Thank you. I'm feeling a little bloated today, so I guess it's a good thing the dress covers that up."

He looks a little confused, but I can't decide if it's surprise over me feeling bloated or because I didn't accept his arm. I want to say, *Hello! I have a skin condition. I'm not blind. I don't need a guide.*

But that would be supremely rude. Though, I'm sure Daimon would get a good chuckle out of it.

We climb the incline toward the village and away from the harbor below. The streets are quiet and the sun is just barely beginning to set on our right, lighting up the periwinkle sky with an amber glow. I sneak glances to my left every once in a while.

Nick is wearing a light-blue Real Madrid T-shirt that hugs his bulging pecs. He's quiet as we cross the street and continue up the road that leads up the hillside. I don't know if he was turned off by my comment about feeling bloated or he's just thinking, but it's making me a bit nervous.

A black man in a black hoodie passes by on the opposite side of the narrow road. It's the same man who passed by the first night Nick came to my door. My stomach flutters with anxiety. Immediately, I begin to have paranoid thoughts that Nick and this guy are working together for some type of law enforcement agency.

But if that were true, I'd already be arrested, wouldn't I?

I take a deep breath to calm my nerves and make a conscious decision to not worry. Turning to Nick, I see he's already casting a devious sideways smile in my direction.

"What are you smiling at?"

He shakes his head. "Nothing."

"You don't have to be shy," I say, nudging him with my shoulder. "Speak your mind."

He looks me up and down a few times as we continue climbing the incline, then he stops walking and grabs my hand to stop me. "Can I ask you a favor?" I stare into his green eyes for a moment before I nod. "Can you pretend to be my girlfriend tonight?"

"What?"

He scrunches his nose in a shameful expression. "I know it sounds weird, but my family has been very concerned about me since I got divorced last year. That's why I'm here. I grew tired of them trying to set me up on dates and giving me pep talks. I was just hoping you could … you know, pretend to be my special friend so they'll stop driving me crazy."

"Your special friend?" His eyes plead with me not to make this so difficult for him and I begin to feel a little bad for questioning him. "I'm sorry. This is just very strange for me. I've never … had a boyfriend. I wouldn't know how to behave."

I stare at the Real Madrid logo on the front of his shirt to keep from seeing the look on his face now that he knows I've never had a boyfriend. I'm not sure what Daimon was, but he definitely wasn't a boy and he was much more than a friend. He was my lover and my enemy wrapped in one tasty package.

"Alyssa?" I look up into his eyes and he's grinning. "You drifted off for a moment. Is everything okay? You don't have to do this. I just thought there was no harm in asking. I'll understand if you don't feel comfortable pretending."

I smile as I realize that I have nothing to be

ashamed of. He's the one asking me to pretend to be his girlfriend.

I let out a relieved sigh. "Sure. I'll pretend to be your *special friend*."

"Are you making fun of me?" he says, continuing up the hill.

"Yes, I'm making fun of you for saying the words special friend."

"How should I introduce you? I can call you my *novia*, which means girlfriend in Spanish. Is that okay?"

I look straight ahead so I don't have to see the hopeful expression on his face as I contemplate this. I don't know how long I'm going to be on this island. Is it wise for people to think I have a boyfriend? It might work to my advantage in keeping creepy men away (for their own good.) But there's always the possibility that I'm being watched. By whom, I don't know.

Part of me believes there's no way Daimon could have survived what I did to him. Another part of me knows I made a mistake that night. A mistake that could have everlasting consequences if Daimon isn't dead.

I shouldn't care what Daimon would think of me moving on with Nick so soon. But I can't help but feel an inkling of hope that I may have misunderstood. Maybe he *did* kill my father in self-defense that night on Hope Street. Maybe my parents *did* kidnap me.

"Alyssa?"

I look up and realize we're standing in front of a small white stucco house with bright blue trim and teak shutters. The sun has set a bit more and half the sky is a dusky midnight-blue while the other half is a brilliant pinkish-gold. Why would anyone ever leave a place this beautiful?

"Is it okay?" he asks again.

I nod quickly before I can change my mind. "Yes, you can call me your nuvia."

He chuckles. "Not nuvia. *Novia.* With an o."

"Yes, that too."

He smiles as he steps toward me and takes my face in his strong hands. Then he lays a soft kiss on my forehead.

"You have so much to learn." He lets go of my face and I feel short of breath as he looks me in the eye. "Come. I want to introduce you to everyone."

As we walk up the front steps, a tall blonde throws the front screen door open, her eyes wide at the sight of Nick. "Nicolas!" she shouts in a gritty Spanish accent.

He smiles at the exuberant greeting as he leans in to hug her. She plants a loud kiss on his cheek and he looks a bit embarrassed as he pulls away.

"*No seas tímido. No te he visto en casi ocho años!*"

She turns to me and holds out her arms for a hug. I give her a limp squeeze and she eyes me warily when she pulls away.

"*Y quien es esta chica?*"

Nick looks at me, smiling apologetically. "She's asking who you are." He turns to the blonde. "*Alyssa es mi novia. No habla español.*" He turns back to me. "Alyssa, this is my cousin Veronica, but everyone calls her Vero."

"*Mucho gusto,*" I say to Veronica with a nod. I do

remember how to say *nice to meet you.*

She looks confused, and rightly so. If he's been here three days, his family has probably already gone to see him in his cottage. And I wasn't there.

We didn't think this through. We'll have to confess the truth soon or this lie is going to keep growing.

Veronica smiles and exchanges a short conversation with Nick in rapid-fire Spanish, then she heads off down the hillside. Nick opens the screen door for me and I step inside, feeling even more intimidated than I did before we arrived.

He closes the door as he enters behind me, then he leans in to whisper in my ear. "Don't worry. My other cousin, Beto, speaks English."

I shoot off a few more *mucho gustos* as we navigate through the crowded living room. Nick explains to everyone that I don't speak Spanish and they all smile and nod at me while trying not to stare too long at my discolorations. I smile and nod back. It all feels so very awkward and forced, until we get to a small kitchen where a young guy is stirring a pot on the stove.

"*Oye, pedo!*" Nick shouts and the guy whips his head around and his eyes light up at the sight of Nick.

"Did you just call him a pedo?" I whisper to Nick.

He laughs and shakes his head. "That means *fart* in Spanish. It's a nickname."

"Fart?"

Nick and his friend embrace and, like Veronica, this guy kisses Nick on the cheek.

"Alyssa, this is my cousin, Beto." Nick introduces us and Beto holds out his hand for a handshake. "Beto, this is my girlfriend, Alyssa."

The lie sounds even worse this time than the last ten times he repeated it.

I shake Beto's hand and he pulls me into a hug. He kisses me on the cheek, his warm lips lingering a bit too long, until Nick claps him on the back.

"Hey, hey. That's enough."

Beto lets go and winks at me. "Forgive me, Alyssa. It's very rare that we get American women on this island." His eyes quickly glance over every inch of my face and hair. "You're quite exotic."

With his dark eyes, messy brown hair, and fair skin, he reminds me a bit of the actor, James Franco. He's gorgeous, though not as good looking as Nick. But the low timbre of his voice is quite mesmerizing. It reminds me a bit of—*No!* I must stop thinking of Daimon. I'm here to have fun.

"I've never been called exotic, but I'll take it as a compliment. Thank you."

"You're welcome. Are you hungry? We have *arepas* and *bacalao.* And if you're thirsty, my Tia Nancy made some delicious *sangritos.*"

"I have no idea what any of that stuff is, but I'll have a drink."

"Good choice!" Beto says, giving me a thumbs-up.

Apparently, a *sangrito* is sangria mixed with mojito: rose wine, white rum, crushed mint leaves, and fresh fruit combine to make a lethal cocktail. After one glass, my face is numb. But I haven't thought of Daimon in at least thirty minutes. So I tell Beto to pour me another.

"How long are you staying on the island?" Beto asks me, handing over the freshly topped off glass of *sangrito*.

I should probably let Nick answer this question, but instead I blurt out, "As long as it takes!"

Beto laughs and glances at Nick. "As long as *what* takes?"

Nick looks concerned. "Alyssa, sweetheart, are you okay?"

I wave off his concern. "Pfft! I'm great."

"Maybe I should take you outside to get some fresh air," Beto offers, resting his warm hand on my bare shoulder.

Nick peels Beto's hand off me and coils his arm around my neck. "I'll take her."

I assume he's going to take me to the backyard, but he takes me back through the front door. Then we start off down the hillside.

"Are you taking me home?" I slur. "I don't want to go home yet."

"I think you should probably rest."

My sandals slap against the pavement as gravity carries us down the hillside much faster than when we ascended. But Nick maintains a firm grip on my hand, and he yanks me back to stop me from plunging into the intersection. The small pickup truck that was about to run me over passes by and I giggle nervously.

"Oh, shit. That was close."

"Too close," he mutters, sounding a bit annoyed. "Come. I'm taking you home."

"I don't want to go home."

I repeat this a few times, imagining it to be some sort of magic phrase, like *there's no place like home*. Only this time, I won't be whisked away to the false safety of my home. This time, I'll be carried away to some place magical and adventurous.

Nick's laughter gets my attention.

"What's so funny?"

"You," he replies, reaching up to brush a piece of hair out of my face. "I get it. You don't want to go home. So I won't take you home. I'll take you somewhere else."

We walk right past Nick's house and my house until we reach a set of stairs that leads down to the harbor below. We pass a few shops and restaurants that are closed for the evening, though one bar remains open and quite lively. We cross through a small parking lot and Nick stops at a guard station near the entrance to the docks.

He carries on a short conversation with the guard, then he leads me down the dark dock. A flitter of movement on my right gets my attention, but when I turn my head all I find is a forty-foot sailboat. I laugh at my paranoia when I see one of the riggings fluttering in the soft evening breeze.

"Where are you taking me?"

"Right here," Nick replies, stopping next to a small rowboat at the end of the dock.

My stomach vaults at the sight of the boat as horrible scenarios play out in my mind. I imagine us rowing out to sea and a storm sweeps us away. Or our boat overturns and we're gobbled up by sharks. Or stung to death by jellyfish.

"No way. I'm not getting in there."

"Don't worry. It's totally safe. I'll get in first so I can help you in. Come." He steps into the boat, then he holds both his hands out to me. "Come closer."

I step forward until the toes of my sandals are hanging over the edge of the dock. Nick reaches up and clasps his large hands around my waist. Then, as if I weigh nothing, he picks me up and sets me down in the boat.

I immediately lose my footing when the boat rocks and I fall back onto my butt. Despite my embarrassment, I laugh harder than I have all night. Nick holds out his hand to help me up, but I wave off his offer of assistance.

"I think I'm much safer down here."

He laughs as he unhooks the rope from the dock and tosses it onto the floor of the boat somewhere behind him. "I think you're right. And I think I'll join you."

I howl with laughter when he plops down next to me, then I scream when the movement causes a small bit of water to splash onto my arm.

"It's just water, Alyssa."

I sit up and the slight rocking of the boat combined with the alcohol sloshing inside my belly are making me queasy. Not one to admit defeat, I grab the two wooden oars lying under my right foot and hand one to Nick.

"Sit up and row," I order him.

He raises his eyebrows at my bossiness, but he can't hide his smile as he sits up across from me so we're knee-to-knee. Then we row. I grip the handle of the oar in both hands and push it forward. It dips into the ocean and I pull the handle backward to propel the boat through the water. It feels good to do something physical, considering all I've done since I arrived on the island five days ago is walk the streets.

About ten minutes later, I begin to feel the burn in my arms and, looking up, I notice we're quite a ways from the docks. The harbor lights twinkle in the distance and the moonlight paints the surface of the water a sparkling silver.

"Wow… Why has it taken you eight years to come back here? It's beautiful."

Nick takes the oar from my hand and, for a moment, I have a weird feeling he's going to throw them into the ocean, along with me. Instead, he sets both oars back on the floor of the rowboat. Then he grabs my hands as he scoots forward a little so one of his knees is between my thighs.

"Beauty appreciates beauty." He reaches up and softly runs his fingers through my white streak of hair, sending a chill through me. "My mother taught me that only beautiful people are able to see the beauty in the world." He delicately traces his fingertips over my cheekbone and down to my jawline. "All this is wonderful, but your true beauty lies inside here." He brings his hand to rest on my chest. "That is what makes you able to appreciate the beauty this island has to offer." He leans forward and lays a soft kiss on the corner of my mouth. "And why this island has so much to offer you."

His other hand lands on my thigh as he kisses

me. And, though his insight on beauty reminds me of Daimon, he doesn't seem to measure up otherwise. I begin comparing the movement and pressure of his lips and tongue to that of Daimon.

Daimon wouldn't swirl his tongue like that. Daimon wouldn't open his mouth that wide.

So stupid. Of course, Daimon wouldn't do any of those things, because he's *dead.*

Nick moans into my mouth as his hand pushes up the skirt of my dress.

I lay my hand over his and pull my head back to stop him. "I think I should go home."

"So soon?"

"Yes."

He sits back and I can't tell if he's disappointed or angry. "As you wish."

He insists on working both oars on the way back, but the movement of the boat begins to make me queasy again. The moment the boat arrives at the dock, I let a stream of vomit loose into the ocean.

"Sorry, fishies," I groan, swiping my hand

across my mouth.

As soon as Nick helps me out of the boat and onto the dock, I vomit again on his Real Madrid T-shirt.

"Sorry!" I shriek.

He smiles as he shushes me. "We have to keep it down. There are people who live on these sailboats. And don't worry about the shirt."

I agree to spend the night in Nick's bed after he explains to me that I can die if I choke on my vomit in my sleep. I don't remember much of the walk up to his house other than my vomiting in front of the guard station and onto the stairs leading up to our street. All I know is that, once I'm lying in Nick's bed, and he spoons me, I forget all about Daimon's kiss.

CHAPTER FOUR

I open my eyes and the sunlight streaming through the window is shining right in my face. A sharp pain pulsates behind my right eye and I hold my hand up to block the light.

"You're awake."

I'm suddenly aware of something heavy draped across my belly. Looking down, I see it's Nick's arm. I turn sideways and he's lying on his belly, his cheek nestled against the pillow, wearing a devilish grin.

A burning sensation builds inside my belly. At first I mistake it for butterflies, but as soon as he moves his arm, I realize I'm going to be sick.

"Where's your bathroom?" I shout my plea as I jump out of bed. "Which way?"

"In the corridor. First door on the left."

I race out of the bedroom and into the tiny bathroom with the gray walls and marble floors. Slamming the door behind me, I kneel in front of the toilet and gag mercilessly. But nothing comes up, save for a mouthful of bitter, stinging bile.

I rinse my mouth and wipe the tears produced by the effort of my dry heaves. I'm never drinking again. Why would anyone willingly put themselves through that? Humans are strange mammals.

I take a deep breath and I can smell the coffee in the bathroom. Nick must be up. Coming out of the bathroom, I put on a big smile when I find Nick standing next to the kitchen counter, pouring some coffee into a green mug.

"Sit down. I'll make you my hangover cure."

"I should probably get going."

He brings me the green mug of coffee and puts his hand on the small of my back to guide me toward the kitchen table. "You need to eat something. I promise. This will kill your hangover."

Kill my hangover, I think to myself as I take a seat. Interesting choice of words.

"I'm really not hungry. You don't have to make me anything. I just want to go home and take a shower. And maybe go back to bed for a while."

"You can take a shower here," he says, taking a skillet out of a cupboard.

"I don't have any clothes. I'll just wait until I'm home."

He chuckles as he grabs a whole slew of ingredients from his refrigerator: eggs, tomato, onion, potatoes, and a few ingredients I don't recognize. He's probably going to make me an omelet. I guess since we're in Spain, it would be a Spanish omelet. The thought of eating eggs right now makes my stomach clench and I take deep breaths through my nose to keep from gagging.

"I'm sorry. I really have to get going," I say, rising from the table and quickly heading for the front door. "I'm not feeling well, but I do appreciate this."

"Wait. I'm—"

"I'm sorry!" I shout as I hurry outside and quickly close the door behind me.

I rush down the paved walkway and out the garden gate, never looking back. The smell of the ocean is like a soothing balm for my lungs. I realize then just how cooped up I felt in that house with Nick.

As I cross the street, I hear footsteps behind me. My heart races as I imagine Nick running after me. I turn around, prepared to tell him to go home, but there's no one there.

Fuck! Now I'm hearing things?

I knew something like this would happen. Living in the dark for so long made my sense of hearing quite acute. Suddenly, my face hurts and tears sting my eyes as an awful question enters my mind. Will I ever get used to living in the daylight? Maybe I'm just better suited for the darkness.

The monsters we can't see are the scariest ones of all.

I knew when my mom said these words to me that she was referring to me. I was the scary monster that no one could see. They hid me from the world to protect others, not just me.

Entering my house, I wipe my tears as I head directly for my bedroom closet to retrieve some clean clothes. I need a shower. I need to wash away the vomit and the salty air that's dried on my skin.

The moment I open the closet door, my stomach drops. That briny smell that was so thick in the air when we were at the docks last night has invaded my wardrobe. But there's another smell mixed in with it.

I sniff the small collection of clothes hanging before me and I immediately recall the scent. Fresh and soapy. Earthy like… oak.

Something in my closet must have come in contact with Daimon while he was in my apartment in L.A. Hell, he was probably in my old apartment many times while I was gone working at the gas station. I've been too busy trying to blend in to my new home, I didn't notice I'd brought a piece of home with me.

I miss L.A.

And, as sick as it is, I miss Daimon.

I miss his scent. I miss his kiss. I miss his voice.

I miss the anticipation of not knowing when he'd arrive. I miss the feeling of his warm skin on mine.

But, most of all, I miss being in the presence of someone who was my equal.

You and I … we are the same, Alex.

I peel off my dress and look down at my perky nipples and the soft curve of my hips. I recall the time Daimon sat me on the edge of my bed and knelt before me so he could devour me. I close my eyes and my heart races as I remember how it happened, allowing my mind to embellish where my memory is fuzzy.

I slide my hand over my ribs and cup both my breasts, pinching my nipples, I imagine Daimon's mouth covering my areola. His tongue flicking my sensitive flesh. That familiar throbbing between my legs returns. A pulsating, flashing signal, beckoning me.

I slide my hand down my belly and into my

panties. As soon as the soft pad of my fingertip comes in contact with my clit I gasp. Leaning against the doorframe of the closet, I inhale that familiar scent as I stroke my swollen bud.

I remember Daimon's mouth sucking my clit. His fingers massaging me from within. How he made me taste myself. Finger-fucking my mouth and forcing me to savor it.

"Oh, God. Daimon," I breathe, my right finger working soft circles over my achingly swollen clit.

I slide two fingers of my left hand into my mouth and imagine Daimon's hard cock. That sticky bitterness I tasted on the tip. My legs begin to wobble as an orgasm approaches. I lift one of my legs and press my foot against the other side of the doorframe across from me to steady myself.

I suck hard on my fingers as my other hand brings me to orgasm. Then I slide down to a crouch on the wooden floor. Hugging my knees to my chest, I finally allow myself to weep for the loss of Daimon.

My other half.

I bury my face in my arms and cry until my chest aches with exhaustion, then a delicate breeze blows over me. Feeling like a soft feather on my shoulder. I open my eyes and find my bedroom window open.

CHAPTER FIVE

After crying for more than an hour, I pick myself up and indulge in a long, hot shower to rid myself of this repulsive behavior. *Fine.* I'm allowed to grieve over Daimon for a short period of time, but I can't draw this out. The man killed my father. I can't indulge in sexual fantasies of the two of us together because, even if he is alive, we will never be together again. If he is alive, the only time I will ever touch him is to break his neck.

His muscular neck with the smooth skin that tastes so… real. So manly.

Oh, God. I'm in trouble. And I'm pretty sure Nick is the only person who can help me.

I try not to cringe as I quickly dress myself in another dress and sandals. I pull my hair up into a ponytail and apply some eye liner and lip balm. Then I sling my camera around my neck and head out the door. Outside, I run into Maria Elena; though she goes by Elena. She's checking her mailbox on the other side of the street.

Elena digs her slender arm inside the box and comes out with a small stack of envelopes. She waves at me as I step out onto the street.

"Hello, Alyssa!" For an older woman, her voice is still quite youthful and melodic. "How are you?"

"Just fine, thank you."

I keep walking toward Nick's house which is right next door to hers and her gaze follows me. "Are you visiting Nicolas?"

I almost blurt out that it's none of her business, but I keep my cool. "Yes, I am."

"Oh, very good. Can you please take this to him?" She walks toward me holding out an envelope. "They put it in my mail."

I take the envelope from her and she tilts her

head as she looks at my skin and my hair. "I can color your hair, if you want. I used to have a salon many years ago, but I still color my own hair."

A sharp pain twists inside my belly and I grit my teeth at that familiar feeling of being judged. "No, thank you. I like my hair the way it is."

"I'm sorry. I did not mean to say that it is not beautiful the way it is."

"It's okay. I understand. And thank you, but I'm not interested in coloring my hair. I'm…" I pause as I try to figure out what the hell I'm doing. "I'm trying to be myself."

I cringe at the irony of telling her I'm trying to be myself when the woman doesn't even know my real name.

She flashes me a warm smile. "Your self is beautiful."

I chuckle softly. "Thank you."

"You should come over for dinner one of these nights. You shouldn't have to eat alone. My husband and I would love to have you." She takes a piece of my hair between her fingers and examines it wistfully. "My children have all moved away. My son is in Barcelona and my baby girl is in Belgium studying. She loves it, but I miss them. I can't really afford to visit them. And they can't afford to come home."

"I will definitely stop by one of these evenings. Thank you for the invitation."

She lets go of my hair and her smile tightens as she realizes I'm humoring her. She tucks her mail under her arm and turns around to leave.

"Wait! Elena."

She turns around, eyebrows raised in a silent question.

I lift the camera from around my neck and hand it to her. "Here. Take this."

"What's this?"

"It's a camera. You can use it to take pictures and send them to your kids."

"Oh, no. I can't take that. It looks very expensive."

"No, please take it," I say, pushing the camera toward her. "Please. I ordered a new one and it should be arriving any day now. Please take it."

"Are you sure?" I nod vigorously and she carefully takes the camera from my hand. "Thank you."

I watch as she heads back to her quaint yellow cottage with the red tile roof. Just one in a thousand other cottages like it on this island. But I'm beginning to realize that each one holds a different story. I think Elena's might be one of quiet desperation. I still haven't figured out *my* story yet.

I knock on Nick's door and he answers almost immediately. He looks me up and down then smiles. It's almost a bashful smile, as if he's embarrassed for making me sick with his cooking.

"I'm starving," I say, holding out my hand. "Can we get some lunch?"

He reaches for me then pulls his hand back at the last moment. "Hold on. I can't forget my phone."

He disappears inside and comes back a few seconds later, tucking his cell phone in his pocket as he pulls the front door closed. He turns around and grabs my hand, swiftly bringing it to his lips and planting a soft kiss on my knuckles.

"I will try not to feel bad that you don't trust my cooking."

"It's not that I don't trust it. I've just had an upset stomach for a couple of days. Just getting use to the island and all."

He casts a suspicious sideways glance in my direction. "I'll pretend to believe that." He begins walking faster until we're jogging. "Come on. The restaurant I want to take you to is always busy for lunch. We have to hurry if we want to get a table."

I laugh as he pulls me to the left at the crossroad and we jog up the incline to a small restaurant with a patio overlooking the harbor. He seems a bit out of breath when we get there, but I could probably go up and down that hill a half dozen times before I'd show signs of fatigue. If Daimon comes back, Nick will be no match for him.

Nick speaks to the waitress, who seems

reluctant to seat us. He seems to be laying on the charm pretty thick, though I don't understand a word they're saying. Finally, her shoulders slump and she nods as she grabs a couple of menus and takes us through the restaurant to the patio.

"What did you have to tell her?" I whisper as she leads us to a perfect location in the corner of the patio where the view is spectacular. From here, we can see the waves crashing against the black ocean rocks below.

"I told her you were dying of cancer and this is your last wish. And…"

"And what?"

He waits until the hostess is gone, then he chuckles. "I told her you are the daughter of a famous Spanish actor. She believed it."

I swallow hard when I think of the words Daimon said to me last week: *You are a princess, Alex! It's time you start acting like one….*

"I'm sorry. Did I upset you?"

I look up and Nick looks worried. "No, no. I'm just thinking about home. Sometimes I get a little homesick."

Homesick isn't exactly the word for what I'm feeling. More like just plain sick of feeling haunted. Sick of feeling anything at all for Daimon.

Nick stares at me through squinted eyes for a moment, as if he's hatching a plan. "I think I can help you with that."

"How? I can't go home — I mean, I can't go home yet. My rent is paid through the month. I need to try to find some inspiration while I'm here."

He smiles and I get a fluttering in my belly. "I think I can help you feel less homesick and help you feel more inspired, at the same time. But I'll have to tell you about it later. I have to talk to—" His cell phone rings and he's almost frantic as he slides it out of his pocket and checks the screen. "I have to take this. I'll be just a minute." He practically leaps out of his chair and answers the phone just as he enters the interior dining area.

That was odd.

The waiter comes by and asks me a question in

Spanish, but I ignore him as I rise from the table and head inside to follow Nick. I see him just as he disappears into a corridor marked with a restroom sign. I hurry over, but I don't enter. I stand off to the side and attempt to listen in, but all I hear is Nick whispering urgently in Spanish.

A woman wearing a straw sunhat looks at me curiously from a few tables away. I must look strange, a half-albino trying to eavesdrop on her date's conversation. I smile at the woman then I flip her the bird and she looks stunned.

"Al—Alyssa?"

Shit.

I turn to my right and Nick has one eyebrow cocked as he waits for me to explain what I'm doing here.

I smile and flip the woman off one more time for good measure. "Sorry, I didn't see you. I was coming to use the restroom and this rude woman was staring at me because I look different. Excuse me."

I push past him and head for the ladies'

restroom. Once inside, I take a deep breath of stale bathroom air and head for a stall. I force myself to piss then I head back to the patio.

Nick looks a bit serious as I take a seat across from him. "I ordered you a glass of wine."

"Thank you," I say, trying to squash the paranoia telling me not to drink it.

We sit in silence for a moment, just watching the waves as they crash against the rocks repeatedly. Finally, the waiter returns to take our order and Nick translates the specials for me. But when none of them sound interesting, he orders something he's certain I'll enjoy then sends the waiter on his way.

"You haven't touched your wine."

"I'm just still feeling a little queasy."

"Queasy?"

"Queasy means sick, to my stomach."

"Oh."

He nods and turns back toward the ocean view. He doesn't believe me. And why should he. He just caught me spying on him.

"Nick?"

He turns to me and raises his eyebrows.

"There's something I have to tell you. I … I left the U.S. to get away from some things … some*one*. I thought he was—"

"You don't have to explain."

"No, I want to explain. I want you to know why I did that." I nod toward the dining area inside the restaurant. "I was burned … badly. In the worst way imaginable. And I'm … I'm scared."

"It's okay. You—"

"I feel like I don't know what the truth is anymore," I continue, not wanting to stop while I'm on a roll. "I used to have a routine. I knew how every day would go from the time I woke up until I lay down to sleep, but now I don't know anything. I don't know who to trust. I don't know if I'll ever trust anyone again." I grab his hand and look him in the eye. "But I want to. I want to let go of the past. I want to trust… someone."

He leans forward in his chair and lays his hand over mine. "I just want you to give me a chance."

He reaches up and cradles one side of my face in his large hand. "Can you give me a chance to show you that I'm not like this person who hurt you?"

A surge of emotion overcomes me and I blink repeatedly to stop the tears from spilling over. The waiter arrives with our food, providing me with a bit of cover to dab the corners of my eyes with my napkin. Once the waiter's gone, I flash Nick a huge smile.

"Let's hurry up. I want to take you back to my place and show you something."

***

We arrive at my cottage, our hunger sated with outrageously succulent seafood. Our thirst slaked with equally phenomenal wine. I feel much better than I did last night after those *sangritos.* In fact, as I close the front door behind me and follow Nick into the living room, admiring his backside view, I'm feeling positively fabulous.

He turns around where the living room and

kitchen meet. "This home has a very warm feeling. Is it just me?"

"No, it's not just you. It's the air conditioner. It doesn't work." I chuckle as I head for the living room window to open it. "This house is 114 years old. Sometimes the water heater doesn't even work and I have to take a cold shower." I unlatch the lock on the window and slide it open. "But at least it has new storm doors and windows."

I flinch as Nick sneaks up behind me and slides his hands over my hips, moving forward until they rest on my abdomen. I can smell his soft cologne as he nuzzles his face in the crook of my neck.

"I've been wanting to touch you ever since I woke up with you in my bed this morning." I close my eyes, trying to ignore that familiar pulsating sensation between my legs as he takes my earlobe between his teeth and gently scrapes them over my skin. "But you left in such a hurry."

A stiff breeze sweeps through the window, lifting the hairs around my nape and carrying with it that familiar scent I've come to associate with

Daimon. His smell must be embedded in this dress from being inside my closet. I glance down and notice my nipples have hardened beneath the thin fabric of my dress.

Though the breeze is cool, my body is warm and receptive from the wine. I want to have sex with Nick. Not just to forget Daimon. I need to feel wanted. I need to be touched by someone other than myself.

I turn around in Nick's arms and press my sensitive nipples into his chest. "Take your clothes off."

He smiles at my order, but he quickly removes his T-shirt. "Your turn."

I peel off my dress and toss it behind him. He coils his arms around my waist and lifts me slightly so he can kiss my burgeoning breasts. His lips on my skin is driving me crazy. I wrap my arms around his neck and lift myself off the ground to wrap my legs around his hips. He kisses me hungrily, our mouths tangled in a wild dance as he carries me toward my bedroom.

"I want to make love to you, Alyssa."

I can't stand the sound of my fake name coming out of his mouth at a moment like this, so I kiss him hard, but he quickly pulls away. He sets me down on the floor next to my bed and grabs my face to force me to look at him

"Do you hear me. I want to make love to you. I don't want to have sex with you." He gazes into my eyes for a while and I feel the moment growing bigger than just the two of us. "I want you to trust me. I can't do this if you don't trust me. I … I adore you. *Te adoro.*"

It takes me a moment to realize I'm not breathing. After a few deep breaths, I wrap my arms around his neck and rest my head on his shoulder so I don't have to look him in the eye when I say, "I trust you."

He kisses the top of my head and moves down, his lips whispering over the curve of my shoulder. I turn my face into his neck and lick his skin, not surprised to find he tastes salty from our day outside in the ocean air. I close my lips around his flesh, scraping my teeth over his skin and pleased to find his cock hardening under his jeans. I slide my hands down and quickly undo his belt and pants, then I push them down hastily.

He chuckles at my urgency as I continue pushing down his blue boxer briefs. "Are you in a hurry, *cariño*?"

The room is darkening more and more with each passing moment. We need to do this quickly before it gets dark. I don't want my first time with Nick to be bogged down by memories of Daimon.

"Yes, I'm in a hurry." I grab his hard length in my right hand and clasp my left hand around the back of his neck to kiss him, but he pulls back. "I have to go to Maria Elena's for dinner," I lie. "She invited me this afternoon before we went to lunch."

"But you just ate. And dinner is not for another four hours or more."

I smile. "Then we'd better get started if we only have four hours."

He laughs, but it quickly turns into a moan

when I firmly slide my fist down the length of his cock. He's not as big as Daimon, but that could be a good thing. Daimon had a way of leaving me feeling absolutely destroyed. In every way.

I slip out of my panties and quickly peel off my bra, then I grab him again. Thrusting my hips forward, I try to rub my clit against the tip of his cock, but I end up smashing his dick.

"*Puta madre!*"

"Sorry!" I cry with absolute mortification. That is not how it happened in my dream.

"It's okay," he murmurs. "Just lay down."

I sit down on the bed then scoot back so I can lie down in the center of the bed. He climbs on top of me, spreading my legs apart so he can settle himself down between my legs. Then it dawns on me.

"Wait!"

"What?"

"Do you have a condom?" I ask, my heart racing as I realize how close I just came to doing something very stupid. I really need to be more careful about these things.

He chuckles as he reaches onto the floor to retrieve his jeans. Digging through the pockets, he finds his wallet and produces a condom from within its folds. He tears it open and my stomach begins to hurt as I watch him slide it onto his erection. This is it. This is really happening.

He kneels between my legs and stares down at me for a moment, admiring my body. I can't help but feel like we skipped a step. I'm pretty sure we skipped the step where he's supposed to make me come first.

Oh, well. I guess if people can kiss differently, then it stands to reason that they also fuck differently.

Ten minutes later, Nick rolls off me, exhausted from thrusting his cock into my pussy. I'm a bit annoyed, but I don't bother bringing it up when he pulls me into his arms to cuddle. I rest my head on his chest as he strokes his fingers softly through my hair.

I sigh as my body begins to relax and I think to

myself, *Sex is a skill that can be learned, right?*

CHAPTER SIX

I feel a little bad about basically kicking Nick out of my bed and my house, but I can't lie here and pretend to trust him. Especially when I'm getting no satisfaction out of it. But as we stand on my front doorstep, the sad puppy-dog look he's casting in my direction sparks something inside me. I just can't figure out if it's pity or genuine affection.

"I'll stop by your house tomorrow morning after I go for my morning run."

"I'll run with you," he counters.

Either this guy doesn't take a hint well or he's trying to keep an eye on me. Either way, I don't like it.

"I'd rather go alone. Besides, I'm leaving really early in the morning. And after I run, I'm going to do some shopping. I won't be long. I'll stop by your place afterward to say good morning."

"*Buenos días.* To say *buenos días.*"

"Right."

He takes my face in his hands and lays a soft kiss on my cheekbone. I hold my breath as he plants another kiss on my forehead, then he kisses me slowly. I can't help but notice that, after just two days together, our kiss has already become synced. Is that all it takes?

It's hard not to feel a little sad and scared about this. Knowing that if I were to kiss Daimon right now, *his* kiss would feel foreign to me.

Must. Stop. Thinking. About. Daimon.

I pull away and quickly turn around to head inside. Closing the door softly behind me, I head back to my bedroom to finish myself off. Afterwards, I shower and change into my old uniform: black hoodie, black jeans, and black sunglasses. Then I wait.

***

I wake at five a.m. and pack a canvas grocery bag with some jogging clothes. Then I dress in my black jeans and hoodie and hope that the weather won't be too hot and humid today. I apply some makeup to cover up my skin discoloration, then I put on one of those uncomfortable brown contact lenses.

I catch the seven a.m. bus to the city and get off on the outskirts of Santa Cruz de la Palma. The buildings are more spread out in this area, but the crime is more condensed. I'm sure if I walk around long enough, I'll find someone who can help me.

Keeping my hood pulled tight over my head, I walk the streets with my head slung low as I watch the activity. A woman hangs up clothes on a clothesline that stretches from her low roof to the top of the block wall surrounding her dilapidated cottage. She eyes me suspiciously as I walk by, but I ignore her and turn right at the corner. A young guy, about eighteen or nineteen, is standing just inside the gate of a small peach-colored house. He stares at me as I pass and I stare right back to show him I'm not intimidated.

I'm almost past his property when he shouts at me, "American!"

I stop and turn around. Unsure if he shouted it as an insult or a question. We glare at each other for a moment in silence, my heart racing as I anticipate whether or not I'm going to have to beat the shit out of this kid.

"Are you American?"

My instinct is to relax when I realize he's just asking a question, but this could be a trick. He may be asking if I'm American so he can rob me. He really doesn't want to try that.

"Yes. Do you speak English?"

He opens the iron gate and steps out onto the sidewalk. "Yes, I speak English."

His hand moves slowly from his side toward his waist.

"You don't want to do that."

His hand stops. "Why?"

"Because I'm an agent with the federal government and I can make your life a living hell." He narrows his eyes at me, unsure whether he should believe me. "Or… I can offer you a lot of money for your help. Your choice."

He clenches his jaw as he contemplates my offer, then he slowly lowers his hand to his side. "What kind of help?"

After forty minutes of Jorge trying to get in touch with various different contacts, he finally finds someone who can help me. We walk the nine blocks to his friend Gringo's house. I don't know much Spanish, but I know *gringo* means white man. So it doesn't surprise me when a forty-something man with blonde hair and muddy grey eyes answers the door of the upstairs apartment.

"Come inside," he says, without the slightest trace of an accent. This guy must be American.

I shouldn't go inside a strange apartment with two strange men. I don't think they'll be able to kill me, but I would rather not have to kill them. Then

I'd have to try to hide out on an island with a population equal to a few L.A. city blocks. Or I'd have to try to escape the island undetected. And that's a bit more complicated than catching a flight out of LAX.

But I really have no choice. I need to know if I can trust Nick or if he's just trying to get close enough to take me down.

I step into Gringo's humble apartment and Jorge follows closely behind me. The living room is clean, with two wicker armchairs and a melon-colored sofa. A glass table in the center of the room displays a dramatic O-shaped wooden sculpture. A sliding glass door is open, letting in the cool morning breeze and the whole apartment smells like coffee. It feels homey and comfortable.

"Have a seat," Gringo says, motioning to one of the wicker chairs.

I sit down, placing my canvas bag of clothes at my feet, and my body tenses as he reaches under one of the couch cushions. I chuckle to myself when he pulls out a laptop and sets it down on the glass coffee table. He sits on the edge of the sofa and opens the computer, tapping on the keys for a bit.

"Okay, I can look the guy up, but I need the cash up front."

"All of it?"

"All of it. Just set it down on the table." I reach for the pocket of my hoodie and within a second, Jorge has his gun pointed at my head. "Slowly!" Gringo shouts at me.

I swallow hard, mostly for affect. Though having a gun pointed at my head does make me a little nervous, I can disarm Jorge and knock both of these bastards out faster than it will take them to piss their pants.

I hold my hands up to show that I'm not concealing anything, then I slowly reach for the wad of cash in my pocket. I place the roll of money equaling seven hundred euros on the table.

"How much is it?"

"Seven hundred."

Gringo flashes Jorge a look of disgust then

turns back to me. "I said one thousand."

"All I have is seven hundred, but I'm good for the rest. I swear."

"I don't give a fuck if you swear!"

Jorge shoves the gun forward until it's pressed against my temple. *Fuck.* These guys are in way over their heads.

"Listen to me," I begin calmly. "I am a federal agent with the CIA. If you kill me, not only will you be arrested, but you'll be tortured by federal agents until you give up everyone you've ever worked with."

Gringo and Jorge laugh at this threat. I take a slow breath and smile as I realize that these bastards think they've got me.

"If you think a federal agent is going to withhold three hundred euros then you're not as bright as I thought. I should just go."

I stand from the chair quickly and Gringo reaches for something underneath the cushion. Jorge adjust his aim, but I twist around and grab his wrist before he can fire. His finger presses down on the trigger and the shot squeals past my shoulder and lands in the flat screen TV on the wall. Gringo retrieves a gun from beneath the sofa cushion, but I twist Jorge's gun around and press my finger over his to shoot Gringo in the chest.

Gringo falls back onto the sofa as Jorge lets go of his gun. I don't want to shoot him, but he's already reaching for the door handle to escape. I shoot him in the head, then I grab the roll of money off the coffee table and my canvas bag of clothes and get the fuck out of there.

I keep my hood pulled tight over my head as I race down the steps of the apartment building. A woman in the apartments below is peering through her screen door to see what's going on. I don't pay her any attention. I keep running for five and a half blocks until I find a bus stop with a bus that's just arriving. I hop inside and head straight for the back.

My heart is pounding like a sledgehammer against my chest. For a moment, I think I might be having a heart attack, until the bus gets about four stops away. Then I begin to breathe easier.

There are only a few people on the bus, so I use the relative privacy to change out of my hoodie and into the running T-shirt I brought with me. That's when I notice the bullet Jorge fired must have grazed my shoulder.

Fuck!

I was supposed to get some information on Nick, and the black guy in the hoodie, then go to the city's free clinic and get a pregnancy test. I'm not very experienced, but I know from watching enough television and movies that a late period often means a woman is pregnant. I'm five days late. Which means, if I *am* pregnant, it's Daimon's child.

The truth is, I never got a gynecological exam when I went back to see Dr. Grossman a few weeks ago to have my stitches removed. And without an exam, she refused to prescribe me any birth control. I didn't want to admit this to Daimon, so I never brought it up. Then I read on the internet that something like fifty-percent of pregnancies end in miscarriage, but most women never know because they think the bleeding is due to their normal period. To me, this meant I had, at best, a fifty-percent chance of getting pregnant. I figured, if I made sure he didn't come inside of me, there would be no chance. Now I just feel like an idiot.

I can't go anywhere in this city now. Not while I'm wearing this clothes and sporting this two-inch bullet graze. I have to get the hell out of Santa Cruz de la Palma.

I ride the bus all the way back to Brena Baja. Then I stop at the corner convenience store to get some laundry soap and first aid supplies. It's about time I washed my laundry in the concrete basin in the backyard. I'm halfway down the street, right in front of Nick's house, when I hear him calling my name.

"Alyssa!"

I sigh and execute a half-turn toward his front door, hoping to conceal the bleeding cut on my shoulder. "Nick! I'm just going home to take a shower. I'll be right out." I start off toward my cottage, then I hear the gate creak as he comes after me. "I really need to shower and get my laundry going. I'll be out in just a bit."

I'm almost to my gate when he wraps his arm around my waist to stop me. "Alyssa, are you okay? What's wrong with your shoulder?"

I clutch my canvas bag to my chest and take a deep breath as I turn around. Looking into Nick's sparkling green eyes, I force myself to become emotional. I mean, a normal person would be hysterical if someone pulled a gun out and nearly shot them.

Jutting my bottom lip out, I sniffle. "I was attacked in the city, by a black man in a black hoodie. I was—" I drop my canvas bag onto the street "—I was so scared, Nick!"

I throw my arms around him and wait for him to stammer as he realizes his partner beat me up. But he just holds me tightly and rubs my back.

"Oh, baby. Are you okay? We're you… I mean, what did he do to you?"

I grit my teeth as I try to come up with a good

story on the spot. "I was in the city shopping and he must have seen my cash and he tried to rob me."

"You were in the city?"

For a moment, I consider lying. He may have heard the news that there was a shooting in the city by now.

"Yes, I told you I was going shopping."

"You said you were going for a run." He lets go of me and looks me up and down, his gaze skimming over my T-shirt and lingering on my black jeans and steel toe boots. "Is that how you dress to go running?"

I snatch my canvas bag off the street and hold it out. "I changed in a restroom in the city, but .... but I was bleeding so much I didn't finish changing. I knew I had to get home quickly."

"Why didn't you go to the hospital?"

"Hospital?"

"Yes, the place where people go when they're sick or injured?"

We stare into each other's eyes for a moment

and I consider blurting out the truth that I was in the city looking for unsavory characters who would help me investigate him using the passport I stole from his cottage last night. But I take a few slow breaths instead as I formulate a better explanation.

"I was trying to get something for you, to surprise you." I reach up, ignoring the pain in my shoulder as I take his face in my hands. "I was on my way to the clinic to get on birth control, so you and I could… you know, whenever we want." My lips hover over his, allowing his craving to grow. "I want to fuck you. All. Day. Long."

I trace my tongue along the crease of his lips and he sucks in a sharp breath before he pulls away. Taking the canvas bag away from me, he nods toward his house.

"Come to my house. I'll help you get that cleaned up."

I glance at the cut on my shoulder then smile at him. "My hero."

He smiles as he leads me back to his house. Once we're inside, he drops my bag onto the kitchen table, then he disappears into the bathroom to get some more first aid supplies that I forgot to purchase at the convenience store. I seize the opportunity to slip the passport I stole back into his desk. I slide the desk drawer closed and when I turn around, Nick is standing behind me holding a bottle of peroxide and some cotton balls.

My heart pounds as he glares at me in silence. I'm about to open my mouth to explain why I was looking in his drawers, but he beats me to it.

"Would you like to go on an American date with me tomorrow?"

His gorgeous lips curl into a smile and I can't help but smile back. "I'd love to."

CHAPTER SEVEN

"Where are you taking me?"

"Shh. It's a secret."

"A secret? I really, really despise secrets," I reply as Nick and I hold hands in the back seat of a taxi.

He squeezes my hand and plants a quick kiss on my cheek. "You'll like this one."

We've been driving north for about ten minutes and I'm getting more nervous by the second. It appears as if he's taking me to Santa Cruz de la Palma — the place where I just murdered two men yesterday. No doubt the police will be patrolling the city. And what if someone on the bus remembers me changing out of a black hoodie. I don't remember anyone looking at me, but you never know. These days, you have to expect that not only is someone watching you, but that they're also taking video to post on YouTube.

"How about we just go back to my house and I'll cook you something?"

He laughs. "I promise this is a good secret."

I grit my teeth at these words. Is there such a thing as a good secret?

It seems the answer to this question is obvious. Yes, of course there are good secrets. The kind that protect people or the kind that result in delayed pleasure. But the kind of secrets meant to protect people are probably the worst of all. You can't protect someone you care about by lying to them.

So it stands to reason that the only good secrets are the ones that are meant to delay or prolong pleasure. If that's the kind of secret Nick has in mind, I can get on board with that.

As we drive through the streets of Santa Cruz

de la Palma, I turn my face away from the cab window, hoping not to be recognized. Nick smiles, probably thinking I can't stop myself from admiring him. Don't get me wrong. Nick is gorgeous. But every time I look at him, I still get that twisting pain in the pit of my stomach. That natural emotion that arises from being so strung out on one human being, anything that reminds you of them just stirs up withdrawal symptoms.

Daimon really did a number on me. He manipulated me by making me feel both beautiful and powerful. By fucking me like he hated me and loved me all at once. You can't fight millions of years of evolution. My female hormones kicked in and tried to convince me to bond with him. Procreate with him. Fall in love with him.

But that's all it was. Stupid hormones. Everything Daimon and I shared teetered on a foundation of deception. I'm lucky it all came crumbling down sooner rather than later. Now I can move on and find out the truth about my past without Daimon's lies poisoning me and leading me astray.

The cab pulls up to a corner restaurant called simply American Bar. I almost laugh at the obvious ploy to attract American tourists, but I'm still a bit on edge from being back in this city and my thoughts of Daimon. Nick pays the cab driver, then we hop out and head for the entrance.

Perhaps for my benefit, Nick speaks to the hostess in English. And I'm not surprised to find she speaks quite well. She barely gives my white face and hair a second glance, then she grabs a couple of menus and leads us to a booth near the window. Nick grabs her hand to stop her before she leaves. He flashes her a warm smile and says something to her in Spanish. I can't believe I'm actually jealous.

She blushes slightly and nods before he lets go of her hand so she can leave. But she doesn't go back to her station near the entrance. Instead, she heads through the swinging door into the kitchen area.

"What did you say to her?" I ask, trying to keep

my voice even.

He grins broadly as he reaches across the table and grabs my hand using the same hand he just used to grab the hostess. "It's a surprise. You'll see."

He brings my hand to his lips and I can feel those female hormones kicking in again, clouding my brain and curling my lips into a bashful smile. I quickly let go of his hand and pick up my menu. Each item on the menu is written in English, with the Spanish translation featured in small letters underneath. It's usually the other way around at the restaurants frequented by tourists.

I already feel better about this American date. I highly doubt the cheeseburgers at American Bar will be as good as the ones in L.A. But at least Nick's intentions seem honorable. He just wants to give me a small piece of home.

Nick insists I order for both of us because I know more about American food than he does. I get us each a cheeseburger and fries, two Cokes, and an appetizer of buffalo wings with good ol'

American ranch dressing. I don't usually eat this kind of junk. In my apartment in L.A., I never really cooked or ate a lot of fast food. I couldn't afford it. I usually ate protein-packed hot cereal nuked in the microwave or homemade turkey sandwiches with no mayo. Sometimes I'd get two-for-one sushi at the Japanese place next door to our building.

Here on the island, the fruits and vegetables and the fresh fish are extremely cheap, so that's what I've been surviving on. I haven't had a cheeseburger or Coke in months. But I guess it's okay to indulge every once in a while.

"So, tell me, Alyssa. What was your life like in the States? Do you have any sisters or brothers?"

I stare at Nick for a moment as I'm overcome with suspicion. That nagging sense that the sunglasses company is just a cover.

"None. And you?"

"None," he replies quickly. "But back to you. What was your life like? The life of a photographer-artist must be quite exciting."

I can feel my top lip trembling under the weight of the lies I'm about to tell. "It's not that exciting. I do most of my work at night, so I've learned to survive on very little sleep. I'd usually gather my equipment and leave my apartment an hour or two before midnight. Then I'd walk the streets waiting for the perfect moment, when the perfect picture would find me."

"That sounds pretty exciting to me. And also pretty scary. You were never bothered? A young girl like you, walking the streets of Los Angeles at night?"

Why is he suddenly so interested in my life in L.A.? I know it's standard procedure on a date, especially an American date, to ask personal questions. We're supposed to be getting to know each other. I understand that. But why does he want to know if I was ever bothered by anyone? That doesn't seem like a normal date question. What if I *had* been attacked, or even raped? Is that appropriate conversation for two people who are just getting to know each other?

"No. I've never been attacked."

"I saw a scar on your…" —he pats his side—"when we made love. Is that from surgery?"

He's asking a lot of questions and I wish I'd found something out at Gringo's house yesterday. Then I'd know whether or not I'm being paranoid. Maybe he's just concerned or genuinely curious.

"It was a work accident. The station was robbed and I got stabbed. Just a hazard of working in L.A."

"The station? Is that some kind of name for your gallery?"

Shit.

"Yes. That's what we call it. The Station." I glance around the restaurant for a moment. "I submit my pieces there and the curator… Ben…jamin puts them on display. He has a few clients who really love my work, so they usually sell pretty quick. But… they do sometimes get robbed."

"That's terrible! They don't have security?"

The waiter arrives with two trays of food. He

places one on the empty table behind me, then he begins unloading the tray in his other hand: two cheeseburger plates and one basket of chicken wings with a side of ranch dressing. He sets the empty tray aside and grabs the other one from the table behind me. My eyes widen at the assortment of drinks and candy on the tray: a bottle of Jack Daniels whiskey; two Snickers bars; a bag of Skittles; and a DVD of *Say Anything*.

The waiter leaves everything on the table then excuses himself. I shake my head as I look at this array of American stuff that would not necessarily be found on an American date, but the DVD shows that he did do at least one Google search. Suddenly, I'm overcome with emotion and regret for having spent the last ten minutes lying to him about my life in L.A.

"Are you… are you crying?"

I sniff loudly and blink until the tears disappear. What is wrong with me? I can't share a meal with him without crying.

"I'm fine. I just… don't think anyone has ever

done anything this corny for me."

"Corny? I'm not so sure, but I think you're saying my surprise is a bad thing, no?"

"No," I chuckle, reaching for his hand. "Not in this case. This is a good thing. You really surprised me. It was a *good* secret."

He smiles and squeezes my hand, but he doesn't look convinced. "Let's eat."

Since I was unable to visit the clinic yesterday, I decide not to have any whiskey. The assortment of junk food and candy is enough to make me sick two hours into our date. But Nick, who found himself to have quite a liking for American spirits, had five shots and two Jack and Cokes. By the time we leave the American Bar, I don't think he can see clearly and his skin looks a bit gray.

I help him into the backseat of a cab and instantly forget about my own upset stomach when he lays his head in my lap. I lightly drag my fingers through his dark hair and the corner of his mouth pulls up in a smile. His arm reaches up clumsily until he finds my hand. Pulling my hand away from his hair, he brings my hand to his nose and draws in a deep breath.

"You smell so good, American girl."

He plants a sloppy kiss on the palm of my hand, then hugs my arm to his chest. I laugh and shake my head, but when I look up, I notice the cab driver staring at me in the rearview mirror.

"*Americana*?" he asks from under his bushy gray mustache.

I nod and pretend to look at Nick so I can keep my head low. He says something else in Spanish, but I don't understand, so I keep my face down and answer with my standard, "*No habla Español.*"

Nick falls asleep on the way home as I gaze out the window at the dazzling night sky. If I weren't so on edge over the cab driver's attempt to make conversation, I'd think this was the perfect end to a fabulous date. Just when the quiet night begins to seep in and relax my muscles, the cab driver turns onto our street. My heart kickstarts when I see a black man in a black hoodie walking down the street past my house.

I ask the cab driver to drop us off in front of Nick's cottage. He's nice enough to help me get Nick into his bedroom. I pay the driver cash and he glances around a bit too much for my taste as he heads back out to his taxi.

Closing the front door, I head back to Nick's bedroom to see if he needs anything, but he looks like he's already asleep. Just to be on the safe side, I crouch on the floor next to his bed and shake his arm a little.

"Nick, do you need anything? Some water, or a bucket, maybe?"

His eyelids flutter open revealing those vibrant green eyes that have been dulled by the whiskey. "Water… and a wet towel, please."

"Sure."

I don't know what the wet towel is for. It must be an old wives tale in Spain or another one of Nick's marvelous hangover cures. I grab a glass of water in the kitchen, then I go to the bathroom to find a washcloth. I run it under the faucet and wring out most of the moisture until it's only slightly damp.

I place the glass of water on the nightstand, then I kneel on the floor in front of him again. Not sure what to do with the cloth, I use it to wipe his forehead. Then I move slowly over his cheek and jaw.

He reaches up and grabs my wrist as his eyes open again. His eyelids flutter under the heaviness of the alcohol, but his lips curl into a sweet, lazy grin. Letting go of my wrist, he reaches out and finds my face. His hand is warm and I hold my breath as I wait for him to say something.

"Thank you."

I sigh and smile back at him. "It's no big deal. It's only fair that the American girl tends to your American bender."

He nods as if he understands, but I'm pretty sure he doesn't. "I love you."

My heart sputters to life, threatening to leap out of my chest. This is not good. This is not a good surprise, at all.

I kiss his forehead and lay the damp cloth on

the nightstand next to his water. "Go to sleep. I'll… I'll be on the sofa if you need anything."

"Don't go. Stay with me."

I swallow hard and brush his hair off his face. "Okay."

I round the foot of the bed and lie down on the other side of the bed, awkwardly staring at the plaster on the ceiling for a moment. Then he turns around and lays his head on my midsection, letting out a big sigh as if *now* he can finally get comfortable.

I run my fingertips over the short hair above his nape, hoping it will help him fall asleep faster. Anything to help him sleep off all the alcohol. To get him back in his right mind.

I don't think he meant to tell me he loved me. It was the whiskey. But if he did mean to say it… That is one secret he should have kept to himself.

CHAPTER EIGHT

Even though I've taken the time to disguise myself, I travel to a clinic on the other side of the island this time. I've been able to hide the scab from the bullet graze underneath my hair, but I don't know how I'm going to explain the new hair color to Nick. First I get attacked in the city, then I dye my hair blonde. If he's not already suspicious of my flimsy backstory as a photographer-slash-artist, then he definitely will be when he sees me today.

But after seeing the same black guy in the hoodie and the cab driver's suspicious behavior last night, I couldn't take any chances. The blonde hair may buy me a few more days on this island, but I'm going to have to leave soon. I may as well find out whether I'm pregnant first. Scratch that off my list. Then I'll know where to go from there.

The taxi drops me off right in front of a small, tan stucco building with the standard clay tile roof. A red and white sign in the window reads *Clínica de Familia de las Cruces*; Family Clinic of the Cross. My Spanish has improved exponentially. I guess it helps that I've had Nick to translate for me.

The receptionist speaks English and she's quite accommodating when I explain to her that I'm American and I'm paying cash. She gets me into an examination room quickly and within minutes, an assistant in pink scrubs comes in with a sample cup for me to pee in. She leads me halfway down the corridor to a private restroom. Without words, she points out the specimen receptacle in the wall where I'm to deposit the cup once I've filled it with urine and wiped it clean. I smile as she closes the bathroom door, then I lock it behind her.

I pull up my orange skirt and slide my panties down, then I sit on the toilet, wishing I'd had the foresight to drink more water this morning. About ten minutes later, I exit the restroom to find the woman in the pink scrubs leaning impatiently against the wall. She was waiting for me this whole time.

She leads me to a nook in the corridor where she sits me down to draw some blood from my arm. Then I'm ushered back out to the waiting room.

The receptionist smiles at me. "It will be just a few minutes. Then they will call you back again," she says cheerily, as if I'm not going to sit here in complete and total agony for the next few minutes.

I grab a magazine off the square coffee table in the center of the room, then I take a seat in the corner and flip through the pages. It's a Spanish travel magazine and I find it funny that they would have this in a clinic in the Canary Islands. One thing you'll find after living in a city for a while is that the appeal of vacationing there diminishes quickly. For instance, I never understood why Los Angeles was such a popular tourist destination. To me, L.A. is a place tourists should avoid. If you want to have fun in California and you want to avoid most of the crime, go to Disneyland or the zoo. But stay the heck away from L.A. and Hollywood.

Not that I've ever been to Disneyland or the zoo. Or Hollywood, for that matter.

Because I was kept in a basement most of my life. According to Daimon, this is because my parents kidnapped me as a child from the Princess of Monaco. I chuckle softly and a woman a few seats away jerks her head toward me, probably thinking I'm a crazy American. She's right. I'm crazy and I may be pregnant with the child of a man who's even crazier.

But is it really so outlandish to believe that my parents kept me hidden for their *own* benefit, and not mine, as they had me believe? No, it's not. Which is why it was so difficult for me to call my mother two weeks ago to confirm my father's death. I expected her to blame it on me and call me an ungrateful monster. But she didn't have much to say to me. I should have expected that.

"Your father has been dead for three weeks. I can't… talk about it. Goodbye."

That was all she said. Luckily, the coroner's office was a bit more forthcoming. My father was drugged and, after a brief struggle, shot in the head.

Since the masquerade ball nearly two weeks ago, I've tried to imagine whether I'd feel any less angry about my father's murder if he indeed had kidnapped me as a child. Would I feel less betrayed by Daimon and more betrayed by my father? I don't know the answer to that question. All I know is that I had about two minutes to contemplate this quandary after Daimon blurted out his accusations at the ball. Two minutes to decide between avenging my father and backing out on my entire plan. I chose to avenge my father, but my desire to back out grew with each passing second that I pressed my foot down on his throat.

It takes four to five minutes of asphyxiation to kill most human beings. A trained assassin like Daimon could probably hold his breath anywhere from four to eight minutes. I blocked off his airway for three minutes because I couldn't stand there for another second. I backed out. Not because I don't love my father. But because I don't know if he ever loved me.

"Aleesa Kendreeck."

I look up to see the girl in the pink scrubs calling my fake name from across the room. I follow her back into the corridor then into another room. She motions for me to have a seat on the examination table and leaves.

Hopping up onto the table, I'm not surprised to find the walls covered with cross-section posters of pregnant women and men with prostate cancer. The room is too cold and the fluorescent lighting is too bright. I find myself wishing I'd worn my jeans and hoodie when my skin begins to prickle with goosebumps. Finally, the door handle turns and a man in a white lab coat and tweed slacks enters.

He stares down at the chart in his hands for a moment, then he looks up, smile beaming as he extends his hand to me. "Good morning, Mrs.

Kendrick. I'm Dr. Hernandez."

I shake his hand and return the greeting without correcting him. If he wants to think I'm a "Mrs." that's fine with me. It's just one more layer of disguise.

He closes the door behind him and lays the chart down on a counter as he continues to leaf through it. "I have your blood work and your urinalysis and I'm pleased to report that you are… a woman." I look at him like he's crazy and he chuckles. "But you already knew that."

"Yes, sir. Can you please just tell me if I'm pregnant?"

He turns back to the chart and scratches his jaw as he flips to the third page. "Yes. You are pregnant."

He looks up again to see my reaction and I can't help but suck in a sharp breath at this news. I hold my breath and let it out slowly, trying to maintain my composure, but I can already feel the tears stinging my eyes.

"I suggest you begin prenatal care as soon as

possible. It appears you are approximately three weeks pregnant. Which puts your estimated due date at 2 February."

"February 2nd?" I whisper. "I can't have a baby on February 2nd."

Dr. Hernandez's eyebrows knit together in confusion. "I'm not sure I understand. But if you need to make arrangements for other… services, we can help you with that."

Other services? Is he asking me if I want to get an abortion?

I have to get out of here.

I thank the doctor and quickly pay the receptionist. Once I'm outside the clinic, I dial the cab company to send another taxi for me.

"Forty minutes!" I yell into the phone, trying not to hyperventilate. "I'm not going to wait forty minutes."

"Miss, you can walk a few blocks south to the hotel Sol La Palma and they have a taxi stand. That is the best I can do."

I hang up and immediately begin walking south

toward the beach, breathing in large gulps of briny air to try to calm myself. What am I going to do? I can't have a baby on February 2nd or any other day.

If my mother drove me crazy, my child will have no hope with a fugitive for a mother. And even if Daimon did survive and I'm not actually a wanted criminal in America, I did kill two men on this island. I'll never be able to go back to the U.S. where I can be extradited. I'll be a single mother on the run for the rest of my life. Even *I* know that's a terrible way to raise a child.

The streets become more crowded the closer I get to the beach and the tourist locations. I pass a small apartment building on my left and I can see the huge Sol La Palma hotel up ahead. Just another block and a half and I can get a ride home.

Maybe I can get Nick to run away with me. Maybe I can even convince him that he's the father of my child. And we can raise the baby together in a villa in South America.

No, I can't expect him to give up his sunglasses company and his family for an American girl he's known for about a week. Though he did say he loves me. Do I really have it in me to ask him to prove it? Do I even want to spend the rest of my life hiding out with a man I hardly know? As tempting as the idea sounds, I'm positive I'm not in love with Nick. And I don't know if I could pretend to be.

I place my hand on my abdomen. Whether or not I admit it to myself or to anyone else, I'm still in love with Daimon. Just the idea of carrying his child fills me with a strange glee. A nervous giddiness that permeates every cell of my body. How sick is that?

I can't even stop myself from imagining he'll be a great father. Teaching our child to be smarter and stronger than everyone else. Like my father taught me.

The horn blares in my left ear, sending a painful shock through my nerves. I'm frozen in the middle of the intersection. Watching in slow motion as the minivan hurtles toward me.

CHAPTER NINE

I brace myself for the impact of the car. In a split second, I imagine the van crashing into the left side of my body, crushing all the bones in my left leg and probably my hip. And my pelvis. Along with every vital organ and microscopic human being held within.

But the impact comes from behind me instead. My body is catapulted forward, my right knee skidding across the asphalt. Then it stops and I can't breathe.

My face is hovering above the hot, dusty gutter and there's something heavy on top of me. And it's moving.

Voices are closing in as a crowd forms around me. I move to try to get a look at the person on top of me. The person who saved me. But something is stopping my head from turning. This person is holding my head still.

"Let me go!" I shout.

In one swift motion, my savior stands up and lets go of my head. I turn onto my back, but all I see is a crowd of people standing over me. They're all looking over their shoulders, no doubt watching as the person who saved me leaves the scene.

"Stop him! Or her!" Why do I want them to stop this person? Whoever they are, they saved me. They did nothing wrong.

Then I smell it. Fresh soap and earthy oak.

I scramble to my feet, ignoring the searing pain in my scraped knee. Pushing my way through the crowd of onlookers, I race toward the direction of their gaping stares. And within seconds I see him. Running toward the hotel.

He seems to be the right height and build. But every time he glances left or right, I can see he has a thick beard. It would be very easy for Daimon to grow a beard in… How many days has it been? Eight? Nine? Is that enough time? It could be fake.

Or I could be desperately grasping for some sign that he's still alive.

I stop in front of a camera store across the street from the hotel and watch as my savior slides into a taxi and leaves in a hurry. If it were Daimon, he would face me. He wouldn't run. Unless the revenge plot he's hatching is much more sinister and involved than a simple showdown on the streets of La Palma. Which would make sense. Daimon knows I meticulously planned his demise. To consider himself a worthy adversary, he would feel obligated to do me the same courtesy of properly plotting my death.

The longer I'm away from Daimon, the more truth I discover in his words. We *are* the same. Even if that wasn't him who saved me, but especially if it was.

***

The entire cab ride back to my cottage, I'm fraught with worry over being thrown onto the asphalt. A spill like that could easily cause a miscarriage. The evil, calculating part of my brain keeps telling me that a miscarriage would be a good thing. It would save me from having to make a difficult decision. But the female hormones coursing through my veins keep screaming at me to see a doctor immediately. Or at least lie down and put my feet up for a while.

I suppose a little rest never hurt anyone. I could use a good *siesta* right now after the morning I've had.

I pay the cab driver and breathe a sigh of relief when I step out onto the street in front of my island home. I'm going to miss this place when I leave in a few days. I'll miss the salty air, the friendly neighbors, and the open-air market. I'll even miss the swollen wood floors and the faulty water heater.

"Alyssa!"

Shit.

I turn around and Nick is waving at me from his garden, beckoning me to join him. Yes, I'll even miss Nick.

"You left early this morning," Nick says, planting a kiss on my cheek as he greets me at the garden gate. "And you dyed your hair."

He smells and looks freshly showered and not at all hungover.

"I didn't want to disturb you. And, yes, I was getting a little tired of the other color."

He opens the front door for me to enter. "Where did you go?" His eyes widen as he looks at my leg. "What happened to your knee?"

I glance down at my knee as I step inside the house. "Oh, it's nothing. I tripped on the curb when I was running to catch a cab. Stupid cab driver pretended not to see me."

I allow Nick to baby me for a bit as he insists on cleaning my wound as I sit on his sofa. "Why were you in the city?"

"I had to get a vaccination." Even I'm surprised

at how quickly that lie came out.

"Vaccination? For what?" he asks, dabbing the scrape on my knee with a wet washcloth. I wonder if it's the same one I used to wipe down his face last night.

"A vaccination to go to Africa. I'm leaving very soon."

"To Africa? Why? For work?"

"Yes. Inspiration calls."

He furrows his brow and sets the washcloth down on the coffee table. Then he picks up a tube of antibiotic ointment and begins dabbing a good bit of it on my knee. Something about this feels very familiar; me on a sofa having my wound cleaned and dressed by a handsome man. My stomach twists at the idea that the twisted string of events I call my life for the past five or six weeks has finally come full circle. Now, more than ever, I understand that I must leave. And I must leave Nick behind.

Nick puts a large bandage over my kneecap, but part of the scrape is still showing on either side.

"I'm sorry, I don't have a bigger bandage."

"It's okay," I reply, patting his shoulder. "Let's go eat something. I'm starving."

So much for resting.

Nick stares at my knee for a moment as he sits on the edge of the coffee table and I see something in his eyes. Something has changed in him.

"Alyssa," he says, looking up and into my eyes. "Would you like to take a trip with me?"

"What? I… I just told you I'm leaving soon."

He takes a deep breath and leans forward, resting his elbows on his knees. "I received an email this morning from a friend of mine in Spain. Is there anything you would like to tell me?"

I narrow my eyes at him, trying to discern where this conversation is going. "No."

He shakes his head, but I can't tell if it's because he's disappointed with my answer or because he's unsure how to proceed. "Alyssa, my friend works for Europol and he tells me that the Prince of Monaco has been talking to American and European law enforcement agencies. He's requesting the safe return of his daughter… Alex Carmichael."

My stomach seizes up and all my muscles tense at the mention of my real name. Either Nick is lying to me about his friend and he's been working his way up to this lie for the past week so he could trap me… Or Daimon was telling me the truth. I'm a princess.

Nick continues, his tone more cautious. "Alyssa, he showed me a picture of this Alex Carmichael, taken when she was boarding a plane in Los Angeles." His eyes flit to my newly dyed blonde hair. "She looks just like you." I move to get up, but he lays his hands firmly on top of my knees to stop me. "Please. I don't want to get in the middle of family business. That's not my intention. I just… I think it's time for you to be honest with me… Please. Tell me what I should believe."

His green eyes are pleading with me to tell him the truth and that's when I realize I can't hide anymore. Everywhere I go, someone is going to find out who I am. As long as I'm running, I'll never be able to be Alex Carmichael again.

But if Daimon was telling me the truth, that means the prince is requesting my safe return so they can kill me. But why would he contact Europol if he were planning to kill me. Unless... Maybe the prince found out his wife was trying to have me murdered. What if he's trying to save me?

No, I shouldn't flatter myself with such dangerous delusions. I have to go to Monaco. I have to kill the prince and princess before they kill me.

"I'll go with you," I whisper, barely able to force the words out of my mouth.

"You will?" He seems almost as surprised as I am.

I look him in the eye and nod. "Yes, I'll go with you to meet this prince. We'll leave in a couple of days."

He smiles and grabs both my hands. "You're doing the right thing, Alyssa. I mean, should I call you Alex?"

"Call me Alex and I'll break your neck." His

face turns two shades whiter, then I chuckle heartily. "I'm kidding. You can call me whatever you want." I lean forward and lay a soft kiss on the corner of his mouth. "Alyssa, Alex, keeper of your heart…"

If these are my last days on this island, I should at least make the most of them.

Nick takes my face in his hands and kisses me hard as he gently pushes me back onto the sofa. I curl my legs around his waist as he grinds his pelvis into mine. He may actually remember to get me off this time.

He slides his hands between my legs and I thrust my hips upward, primed to receive his touch, but all he does is push my panties down.

"No. Get up," I say a bit too impatiently.

"What's wrong?"

I push his shoulders back and it takes him a moment to get the hint. He sits back on the other end of the sofa so I can sit up. I have half a mind to tell him he's doing it wrong, but I can't. Our last days on this island are supposed to be pleasant.

Besides, I'm pregnant with another man's child. I can't have sex with Nick. Wouldn't that make me a whore? Even if Daimon is dead, he's dead at my hand. So, technically, that would make me a black widow.

"I'm sorry. I'm just dying to take a shower and a nap. I was a little worried about you choking on your vomit last night, so I didn't get much sleep." I stand from the sofa and he stands after me. "I'll be back later. Or you can come by my place in a few hours."

He looks a little dissatisfied with this explanation, and with my leaving him with a throbbing bulge in his pants, but he just nods. "Whatever you say. I'll come by later to check on you."

We say our goodbyes and I hurry home. After a quick shower, I don't bother reapplying any ointment or bandage to my scrape. I just dab it dry and slip into a nightgown. Then I curl up in bed, hugging my pillow between my thighs.

"Where are you, Daimon?" I whisper my plea

to the bedroom window. "I'm pregnant."

I adjust the pillow between my legs and the friction sends a tiny shock of pleasure into my clit. Closing my eyes, I imagine it's Daimon's bulge, which is a bit more impressive than Nick's. I wrap my legs around the pillow as I slide it back and forth.

"Oh, Daimon," I breathe, imagining Daimon's jeans popping at the seams over his hard cock.

Up and down, forward and backward, he grinds into me until he can't take it anymore. He must taste me.

I kick off my panties and spread my legs wide, then I reach for my throbbing clit.

"Oh, God! Daimon!"

My hips buck against his mouth as he licks me up and down then in a slow swirling pattern. Oh, that tongue. That beautiful tongue.

"Yes, Daimon. I'm coming."

My body convulses and as my pussy clenches intermittently, releasing a river of juices for Daimon. I take a moment to collect myself, then I roll onto my side and pull the covers up to my chin. I need to get some rest. Maybe I'll just stay in bed all day.

Tomorrow, I'll spend my last day on this island with Nick. And I'll make love to him, whether he makes me come or not. Because life isn't always about what you can get. Sometimes you have to give more than you receive.

Then we'll leave for Monaco. Nick will imagine a beautiful reunion. While I imagine something a bit more bloody.

Alex Carmichael is dead.

Daimon Rousseau may be dead.

But after tomorrow, the Prince and Princess of Monaco will definitely be dead.

CHAPTER TEN

I cut through the neighbor's backyard to get away from Alex's cottage. I'm not surprised to find eighty-year-old Ignacio pulling weeds in his strawberry garden.

"*Hola*, Ignacio!" I shout to him.

He straightens out his crooked back and turns toward the sound of my voice. Flashing me a glorious toothless smile, he waves vigorously. He doesn't know my name, so he doesn't return the greeting verbally. All he knows, from the first time I passed through here last night is that I live on a forty-foot sailboat in the harbor on the other side of the island. And that I'm in love with the new girl next door.

I had to be up front with him about this. Then he wouldn't mind me cutting through his backyard every once in a while. Everyone understands a person in love acts irrationally.

Which is why I've given Alex the benefit of the doubt that she purposely left me alive. If she had wanted to kill me, I'm certain I'd be dead. And what I've seen while observing her so far only solidifies this theory in my mind.

Alex knew exactly how to kill me without leaving any evidence. The plan she executed at the masquerade ball was not something the average woman her age could pull off. Her only mistake was believing she could set aside her feelings for me long enough to follow through with her plan. Well, that was her second mistake.

Her first was watering down the tranquilizer so she would have time to divulge her plan to me before I fell unconscious. She watered it down too much. I had to pretend to be unconscious, then I had to hold my breath for three minutes and pretend to be dead. I was drowsy enough that I couldn't fight her off. And I was lucky enough that the drugs slowed my heart rate and weakened my pulse. In her distraught state, she was sloppy when checking if I was truly dead.

After she left, I assumed she would go straight to the airport. So I stumbled out of the hotel and caught a cab to her apartment. The detective in me needed evidence. I needed to know where she was going so that when the drugs wore off, I could find her and make her pay. I didn't expect to walk into her apartment and hear her sobbing in the shower.

I almost walked into the bathroom and told her I'd forgiven her, but I kept imagining my fingers wrapped tightly around her throat. I knew I had to leave before I did something I would regret later.

Searching her apartment, I found a laptop under her bed with all her flight information. I emailed the itinerary to myself and wiped her hard drive. Then I went through her trash and found the fruit that I had given her. It was just too tempting not to put it back in the fridge to send a message.

I'm convinced Alex knows I'm still alive. In a sick way, Alex needs me as an adversary as much as she needs my cock inside her. As the Americans say, she wants her cake and eat it too.

Well, I am more than ready to give Alex the whole fucking cake, and the cock. But first, I need to make her pay for almost killing me. She's young. She has many lessons to learn. And I'm going to have a lot of fun being her teacher.

I understand the cruelty in making her pay for a crime that was meant as retribution for my own crime, but she doesn't understand what happened with her father. The truth is that her father's death was completely unnecessary. Some of it was error on my part, but mostly it was his own stubbornness. I underestimated the old man's prowess. He may have been forty-nine years old, but he had a lot of fight left in him from his army days. I should have known this, after the months of research I did on Alex and her family.

I wasn't supposed to do any research on this job other than Alex's daily habits. But watching her live her life in the dark sparked my curiosity. I had to find out more. And that's when I found she'd been treated like a dirty secret for most of her life.

What kind of parents keep their daughter hidden in a dark basement for eighteen years? Their entire house was void of any evidence they even had a child. This madness and the fact that the Princess of Monaco wanted her killed, turned Alex into a mythical figure in my mind. Why would anyone want to hide her away? And why did the princess want her dead?

None of it made sense. Until I traced the curves of Alex's mouth with my finger and discovered I'd traced those same lips before, with my tongue, when I fucked the princess.

It's not something I'm particularly proud of. But a forty-two-year-old ex-supermodel is still a very sweet conquest. And I'd never been with a woman twelve years my senior. I'm always willing to try something new. It's hard to say no when your new boss tries to seduce you. Especially when she is promising you a $20 million payday.

But I do regret it now. Now that I know why she wants Alex dead. Alex is the princess's dirty secret. The stillborn she supposedly had nineteen years ago wasn't actually a stillborn after all. It was Alex. And Lisa Carmichael, the woman Alex has called "mother" all her life, is actually the midwife who helped deliver her.

Lisa was supposed to take newborn Alex to a local hospital and claim to have found her abandoned near a dumpster. But Lisa had something else in mind. She kept Alex hidden until she and her husband, Joe Carmichael, could get certified as foster parents. Then she mysteriously found a four-month-old baby behind the hospital. They took Alex in as their first foster child and eventually adopted her. That's when Lisa started blackmailing the princess.

When Alex turned eighteen, the princess refused to make her annual extortion payment. That's when Lisa and Joe got desperate and their greed drove Alex away. Which only presented the perfect opportunity for Princess Amica to finally get rid of her dirty secret.

The only thing standing in her way was her ex-Black Ops father who never let Alex out of his sight.

That's when they called me.

I come out onto the street where the open-air market is lively with merchants and patrons haggling over fish, produce, and textiles. Since I arrived on the island yesterday, I've taken the time to acquaint myself with almost everyone in the town of Los Llanos on the other side of the island where I keep my boat docked. You never know when someone will turn from acquaintance to ally.

I continue down the narrow street until I pass the last booth in the market and come upon a fishing supply store. A bell rings when I enter the shop and the young girl behind the counter looks up from her magazine.

"*Buenos dias.*"

She casts a bashful smile in my direction as she closes her magazine and sits up straight. "*Buenos dias, señor.*"

Her light-brown hair hangs over her shoulder in a messy braid and her green eyes are practically flashing signals at me. She looks like a sweet girl who probably just wants to be fucked by a foreigner, but I'm not interested. She's pretty, but she's not my Alex.

I flirt with her a little so she gives me the fresh bait from the tank in the back of the store. Mackerel are actually quite delicious to eat. They're not just bait for larger fish.

I take the bag of mackerel from her and flash her a warm smile. "*Gracias.*"

She leans over the counter, trying to show me her cleavage. "*Hasta luego.*"

I head out and through the market again. Alex will no doubt be taking a long nap right now to rid herself of the impure thoughts she's having of me. So it should be safe to walk down the street. Not that she'd recognize me.

I've grown my usual four days of scruff out to a thick eight-day beard. And I've changed out of the clothing I was wearing when I had to save her life this morning. Now I'm wearing a tourist T-shirt, khaki cargo shorts, sunglasses, and a fisherman's hat.

As observant and vigilant as Alex is, she misses a lot of obvious signs that she is being played. She didn't know that I was watching her right now as she screamed my name while caressing her wet pussy. That was quite a show.

It was difficult not to climb in her window and fuck her properly. It's even more difficult not to get in there and taste her. My craving for her is so strong it's painful. But I can't make my presence known yet. I have to debrief Crow and set my plan into motion first.

Crow has been keeping an eye on Alex for me this past week while I was in Monaco. And I do not like the news he's given me about this new romance she has herself caught up in. Nicolas Costa.

I chuckle to myself as I pass the convenience store at the end of the street. All Alex has to do is think of me and she comes. According to Crow, poor Nicolas couldn't even get past first base when Alex was drunk. He's a pathetic excuse for a man. And an even more pathetic excuse for a bounty hunter.

But I'm not worried about Nicolas hurting Alex. And I'm even less afraid of Alex falling for Nicolas. Alex will be mine again. I just have to make sure I approach her cautiously and at precisely the right moment. The only problem is I've been given a deadline.

Since I failed to deliver on my promise to kill Alex in Los Angeles, I've been given two weeks to kill her in La Palma. And my old friend Crow is eager to finish the job for me if I fail again. Twenty-million dollars is a lot of money. Even in the assassination business.

What they don't know is that I don't have two weeks. I have only one day to convince Alex not to get on that plane with Nicolas. I don't care if the prince is genuinely working against his wife in an attempt to keep Alex safe. Crow won't allow Alex to step off that plane in Monaco for a beautiful reunion with her biological father. Crow will take down that plane and every person on it to get that twenty-million.

When I turn onto Dolores Street, I'm pleased to see Nicolas working out his sexual frustration in his garden. I cross the street with a spring in my step and stop next to his gate.

"*Hola, amigo!*" Hello, friend.

He looks up from the dirt he was just probing with his shovel. "*Hola.*"

I proceed in Spanish and, I must admit, I'm quite impressed with my proclivity for foreign languages. "I noticed you moved in recently and you've already found yourself a beautiful friend from across the way."

I wiggle my eyebrows, though I'm not sure he can see it under my sunglasses. His lips turn up slowly in a wary smile.

"Yes, do you know Alyssa?"

I shake my head. "No, sir. But if you really want to impress her, I have a boat you can charter." I draw my knife out of my holster and use it to point toward the harbor where I'll be mooring my boat later night. "If you'd like to take it out for a little while, I'm sure your girlfriend would find it very romantic. I'll give you a special rate, since you're my neighbor."

Nicolas eyes the knife in my hand with even more unease. "Thank you, friend. I'll keep that in mind."

I give him my number then he continues digging his hole in the ground. I smile as he bends down and scoops up a dead crow. He drops the bird into the hole and begins piling the dirt on top of it.

"Watch out for those crows," I call out. "They're everywhere."

***

I slap the two-pound sea bass onto the counter in my small galley kitchen. Sliding my boning knife into it's belly, I cut it open and smile as the blood runs out onto the plastic cutting board. I rip out the guts with my hand and throw them into the waste bin at my feet.

As much as I don't want to think about Carla, preparing my own dinner always makes me think of the night she left. I knew she was planning to leave me. But I couldn't bring myself to care.

It had been one and a half years since I gave up my job as a hit man. I had just began working for the Los Angeles Police Department. Carla and I had moved into our apartment in Venice Beach recently and, all circumstances pointed to us having a happily ever after. But I was not a happy man.

Not only was I no longer doing the job that made me who I was, I was still grieving the results of my final job as a hit man. The only thing that made me feel partially alive was chasing a perp or fucking a beautiful woman. Carla was beautiful, but she wanted more from me than just a fuck. She wanted something I couldn't give. And, after a hundred discussions about our future that went nowhere, and the countless disgusted looks she cast in my direction whenever she found empty condom wrappers in my pockets, she finally got fed up.

After I clean and sauté the fish, I sit down on a bench seat on the deck with my dinner plate and my glass of local wine and I watch Alex's cottage. Moving the boat to this side of the island is part of the plan. As I finish my last bite of sea bass, Nicolas arrives at her door. Checking in on her to make sure his bounty doesn't slip through his fingers. Maybe he'll pretend he's checking to see how her knee is doing.

I really should have stopped her from going into that clinic today. I would have preferred for her to find out she's pregnant after I make my presence known. I don't like having an unfair advantage. But the truth is that the child inside her, our child, will make our reunion that much more interesting. No doubt she'll be angry when she sees me. She'll be tempted to risk her life and the life of our unborn to make me pay for my sins. But I've seen the softer side of Alex. The part of her that wants nothing more than to be touched, cherished, loved. She knows she can have all that and more with me.

My chest floods with violent rage as I watch Alex open her front door and invite Nicolas inside. The thought of his hands and lips on her is the worst part of this whole mission. I want to slowly break every bone in his body and watch him writhe in pain for even *thinking* he could touch her. But, once again, patience is a virtue.

I must wait for the right moment. Alex is carrying my child. Which means I'll do anything to keep her. I'll endure any agony to get her back. I'll kill anyone. I'll agree to any of her demands. But I need her to forgive me first.

Forgiveness.

Such a simple word with such complicated and varied implications depending on who you ask. What is forgiveness? Does it mean you forget the wrongs committed against you? Does it mean you embrace your tormentor?

I wish I knew. The answers to these questions become even more murky when the person you need to forgive is yourself.

I wash the dinner dishes and shower, then I get dressed to head out on patrol. Lurking in the shadows, collecting intelligence and investigating every lead is part of who I am. It's why I was such a great detective. And why I was an even better hit man before that. It's why Princess Amica contacted me first when she needed Alex killed.

It's too bad that she caught me at a very low point in my life. If I had been high on another kill, I may have taken Alex out, no questions asked. But I hadn't taken a job in three years. Though I fantasized about leaving the L.A.P.D. and going back to my old life, I couldn't bring myself to do it.

I hesitate to describe myself as broken. Broken people don't have the capability to put themselves back together. But that's what I did over the last few months as I investigated Alex and her family. In learning Alex's story, I learned that I was not alone. And maybe, if I wasn't alone, I still had hope.

I slide my .44 Magnum out of a drawer and

hold it in my hands for a moment, lost in thoughts of the last time I used this gun for a hit.

I'd been working as a self-employed hit man for two years after leaving the Central Directorate of Interior Intelligence in France, more commonly known as the DCRI. I was working on high-level counterintelligence operations and realized my biggest thrill was taking out the bad guys. But not just taking them out. I took pride in completing each job without collateral damage. But that all changed on a warm August evening three years ago.

I was sent to London to take out a CIA operative who had gone rogue on a counterterrorism operation. I was hired to take him out before he was caught and tortured into giving up his secrets. He'd been in hiding for three months, but my intelligence had placed him in a small flat in West London. His family wasn't supposed to be with him that night.

Even three years later, it still makes me sick to my stomach. I can't get the image of that little boy dead, looking so peaceful in the comfort of his father's arms. I had come into the man's bedroom while he slept. As he lay on his side sound asleep, I put one bullet through his back, where his heart would be, and another bullet in the back of his head. The first bullet ripped right through his chest and lodged in his son's brain. His son was snuggled up against him underneath the covers.

I tuck the .44 into the waistband of my shorts and pull my T-shirt down. Looking at my reflection in the porthole, I scratch my jaw and muss up my hair before I pull on a baseball cap. Turning away, I slide my sunglasses over my eyes.

I am not a good man. But Alex and our child are my chance to redeem myself. I just need to convince her that we are safer together. Because she'll never be safe as long as there's a hit on her head.

It took a lot of sweet talking on my part to get Princess Amica to agree to let me finish this job. She wanted to hand the job over to my friend, Crow, but as the only other person who was there with me that night in London, he knows I won't give this one up. He knows I wouldn't have come out of retirement for just any case. There may be no loyalty amongst thieves, but there's a different code of ethics for hit men. Crow remains loyal to me.

But $20 million is a lot of money. He's still hanging around the island, helping me with intelligence and waiting for me to screw this up so he can step in and finish the job. I don't care how many years we've been friends, if he so much as breathes on Alex, I will gut him faster than a sea bass.

The image of that dead boy's face flashes in my mind again and I take a seat at the small table near the galley kitchen. I grit my teeth against the memory and the mental self-flagellation that always follows. The inner voice telling me I don't deserve to live after committing such a heinous act. That child didn't deserve to die.

I went three years barely clinging to a long list of excuses to keep on living. It wasn't until I started following Alex that I began to see what my purpose is. My purpose is to save her. To love her. And I will stop at nothing to do just that.

***

The Arkham Bar is housed inside a small, blue building with a clay tile roof. It has a warm, Spanish-island feel on the outside, but the modern, artsy interior feels cold. I feel a bit exposed in this tiny place, but that's why I brought Crow here. Because if I feel a bit exposed, he's going to feel downright naked.

The bartender asks for our drink order as soon as we take our seats in the uncomfortable white barstools. Crow keeps his black hoodie pulled tightly around his face as he sits next to me and we both order an Alhambra lager. We wait in silence as he retrieves the beers from a cooler under the bar and flips off the caps before he slides them to us. I pay for the beers and tip the bartender generously, then I let him know we're not to be interrupted.

"If you didn't want to be interrupted, you

should have chosen a different fucking bar," Crow complains in his British accent. "I look like a fucking wolf in a hen house here."

"Don't worry about maintaining a low profile in this bar. Worry about it when you're out there walking the fucking streets. How many times has Alex seen you?"

He takes a long pull on the bottle of beer to make me wait. "I don't know and I don't care. If your girlfriend is feeling the heat, then she's got good fucking reason to. She's getting impatient."

He's referring to Princess Amica growing impatient waiting for me to get Alex out of the picture. "I don't give a fuck if she's getting impatient. I have to do this my way."

He chuckles. "And your way is to have a go at her first? Fuck her body and her mind then kill her. Is that it?"

"You don't know enough about my strategies to question me."

"I know your strategies don't always work."

I should crack his skull for that comment, but I

can't. I need to keep Crow close, where I can keep an eye on him. I'll take his snide comments about how I fucked up my last job. But once I have Alex back, safe in my arms, he's on his own.

This is a not a business for making and keeping friends. Crow and I stumbled upon a friendship when I passed up a job due to a booked schedule. I'd been taking out marks for more than a year and my services were in high demand. It was Crow's second job, and he came to me asking for advice. Two years younger than I was and thirsty for blood after a tour in Iraq, it was difficult not to feel sorry for him.

I took him under my wing and brought him along on my last two jobs. I owe him my life for getting me out of that London apartment when I was too stunned to move. But he's the one who screwed this up with Alex. He had to throw that fucking cigarette butt onto the street when he was following Alex on Hope Street. If she hadn't found that, she wouldn't have found out about her father so soon. And I might have had a chance to tell her when she was ready.

Crow knows he fucked up, which is the only reason he refused to take the job off my hands when Amica wanted to hand it over to him. Now he thinks I'm trying to prove myself, but I have nothing to prove to him or Amica. Alex is the only person I need to prove something to.

"What is her schedule like? Is she going to the Billionaire Club next week?"

Crow looks at me sideways as if he knows what I'm thinking. "Don't think of throwing away this payday for that girl, Daimon."

"I can't tell you what I'm planning. But it has nothing to do with that fucking $20 million. What I have in mind will be much more lucrative, for both of us."

"Both of us meaning… you and *me* or you and the girl?"

"You and me. I just need to get that fucking bounty hunter out of the way without raising any red flags with the local law enforcement. It will be done soon."

He downs the rest of his beer, but he still holds it close to his chest as he contemplates this. "She's giving you three days to make it happen. And so am I." He lets go of the beer bottle and slides off the barstool. "This better be good."

I smile as I realize he doesn't know about Alex and Nicolas's plans to fly to Monaco in less than two days. Typical Crow. Always one step behind when he thinks he's one step ahead.

The bartender brings me another beer, as if he can sense that I need it. I sip it slowly as I contemplate my options here. I need her to start believing me and questioning her parents, otherwise she may try to kill me again. And I'm done underestimating her.

I'm through underestimating everyone.

I never imagined that Princess Amica had hired me to kill her own biological daughter. But I should have known that there was something far more mysterious about Alex from the moment I stepped inside her adoptive parents' home. Which brings me to my other predicament: Keeping Alex's mother, Lisa, alive.

I had Crow watching over her when we were in L.A. But now that we're both here in La Palma, I had to hire another man to keep watch over her.

Lisa Carmichael is surviving in the basement of their home, just the way they made my Alex live for eighteen years. The plan was to have both Lisa and Joe down there, to get Joe out of the picture so I could get to know Alex and see if I could indeed go through with the hit. But Joe refused to be confined. Then he escaped. In my fucking Mercedes.

A girl in a blue tube top and white shorts sidles up next to me at the bar and asks for a draft beer. She smiles at me and I turn back to my bottle. Downing the rest of the beer, I slam it down on the bar and head for the exit. If these girls knew Alex, they wouldn't bother. If they knew the kind of woman they were competing with, they'd cower at her feet.

No one can compare to my Alex. There is no way I could ever enjoy being with another woman now that I've had a woman like her. And for a man like me to swear off all women for one girl, I'd have to be insane or in love. Or both.

I step outside into the warm island air, smiling as I gaze at the stars. By this time tomorrow night, I'll know whether Alex and I are going to spend the rest of our lives together or kill each other.

CHAPTER ELEVEN

I take my time packing all my clothes. Though I'll probably leave all my luggage and belongings behind after we land in Monaco and I kill the royals, I'm savoring this alone time while Nick and I are apart. He's in his cottage packing. He's not around to watch as I sniff the pieces of clothing that still smell like Daimon, one by one before I lay them down in my suitcase.

When I'm done, I zip up my luggage and look around the bedroom. I walk to the window and push aside the sheer curtains to look outside. I can see my neighbor Ignacio working on a wooden worktable in his backyard. He's loading his shotgun and preparing his ferrets to go rabbit hunting. He looks up briefly and I take the opportunity to wave at him. He smiles and waves vigorously, then his gaze slides off to the side. I move forward to look outside, but I hit my head on the glass. I look up and Ignacio's wife, Noemia, appears at his side. She squints at me for a moment, then she waves. I'll miss the Spanish music and delicious smells that wafted out of their window as Noemia cooked.

"Are you ready?"

I whip my head around and I let out a sigh of relief. "You scared me. Your voice sounded different."

Nick smiles and holds out his hand, his other hand tucked behind his back. "Come. I have a very special surprise for our last day in La Palma."

He's wearing a nice pair of black slacks and a white dress shirt with his sleeves rolled up. This is a very good look for him.

"Did you say goodbye to your family?" I ask, taking his hand and leaning back to try to peek at whatever he's hiding.

"Yes. And they're very pleased to know that I'm leaving the island with you. They are very fond of you."

Very special surprise… very pleased to know… very fond of you…. Either he's buttering me up for something he's not sure I'm going to enjoy or he's actually nervous. I'm pretty sure it's the former and not the latter.

"What are you hiding back there?"

He pulls his hand out from behind his back, brandishing a bottle of red wine. "My great-uncle gave me this for us to celebrate our last night in La Palma. It's a *gran reserva rioja* from his vineyard. Twenty-three years old and at its peak."

"Wow… Sounds like I should be impressed."

He lets go of my hand and opens the front door for us to exit. "Tonight, we dine like royalty." My smile evaporates into the humid evening air and he quickly realizes his gaffe. "Sorry. I didn't mean that the way it sounded."

"It's okay. I'm sure I'll have all the guys vying

for my hand now that I'm a princess. You'll have to work a lot harder to impress me after tonight."

"I accept the challenge, your highness," he says, getting down on one knee and bowing his head dramatically.

"Stand up. You're embarrassing me."

He chuckles as he gets up. "Why? There's nobody out here."

I smile and take a quick glance over my shoulder at Ignacio and Noemia's house. The front of their house is empty but for the dark shadows of night crawling over the concrete porch. They're still in the backyard. Then why do I feel so uneasy, as if I'm being watched?

"Are you okay?" Nick asks, holding out his arm for me.

I link my arm through his and we set off down the street toward the harbor. "I'm fine. Where are you taking me? Another boat ride?"

"Yes, but this time I've got a much bigger boat."

"A much bigger *boat?* Sounds like I'm in for

quite a ride."

He laughs and leans over to kiss my temple. "You have a dirty mind, *cariño.*"

"You have no idea," I mutter to myself, thinking of the multiple times I've pleasured myself to thoughts of Daimon.

"What did you say?" he asks as we descend the stairs from the street down to the harbor.

"Nothing."

We arrive at the harbor and I immediately notice that there's a different boat docked here than the last time we came. This sailboat is a bit bigger than the other one and this one seems to be stocked with servants. A crew of three men stand on the deck smiling down at us, while another gentleman stands next to a stairway, which has been unfolded to meet us on the dock.

"*Buenas noches, Señor Costa,*" the gentleman on the dock says, waving his hand toward the staircase leading up to the deck. "*Todo está listo para una gran aventura.*"

"What did he say?" I ask Nick as he leads me

toward the steps.

"He said everything is ready for a grand adventure."

I climb the steps toward the deck, wondering why I'm feeling creeped out by the wide smiles plastered across the faces of the boat servants in their tuxedos. But I'm not exactly used to being treated like royalty. And I don't think I could ever get used to this.

One of the men who is possibly a waiter, leads us to the front of the boat where a table dressed in white linen and set with elegant tableware for two awaits. He takes the bottle of wine from Nick and slips a corkscrew out of his pocket to open it. After he pours us each a glass, he nods and excuses himself so Nick and I can be alone.

Nick grabs both glasses and hands me one. "To a pleasant reunion with your parents and—"

The boat begins pulling away from the dock and the inertia pulls us both backward. Nick catches me before I tumble onto the dining table, but I still manage to spill a good bit of red wine on the white tablecloth. I grab a napkin, dipping it in the glass of ice water on the table, then I attempt to remove the stain.

Nick clamps his hand around my wrist. "Leave it. They'll wash these later. Come."

I leave my glass of wine on the table and follow him toward the front of the boat. Grabbing the railing, I close my eyes and breathe in the fresh air. The air smells better at night, once most people have pulled their smoggy cars into their driveways and the winds have died down. The late evening is when you can fully appreciate the scents of nature as they settle and unfurl all around you. God, I miss walking the streets at night.

Nick downs his entire glass of wine and tosses the glass overboard. Then he presses his chest against my back, placing his hands on the railing on either side of me, caging me in. His lips graze the back of my ear and I suck in a sharp breath.

"Maybe we should sit down," I whisper, my voice barely audible over the roar of the water as the boat is propelled forward.

His tongue darts out, tracing the shell of my ear as his right arm curls around my waist, pulling my backside flush against the bulge beneath his slacks. His fingers curl around the bottom of my shirt as he slowly lifts it up then slides his warm hand inside the waistband of my skirt.

"What are you doing?" I whisper a bit louder this time.

"I'm going to give you a grand adventure."

His hand slides lower until it's inside my panties. He fumbles around a little, pressing on the wrong places until he finds my opening. He slips his thick middle finger inside me and grunts in my ear.

"What's wrong?"

"You're not wet."

I'm about to reach for his arm to pull his hand out of my panties when he moves his finger and finally finds my clit. "Oh, God."

He chuckles softly. "There it is."

I grip the railing, knuckles white as he strokes me slowly. This is so much better than doing it myself. I twist my head around, then I reach back to grab his neck and pull his mouth to mine. He kisses me hard as he caresses my clit and I forget about everything and everyone else around us. Grinding my hips in sync with the rhythm of his hand, I moan louder with each passing moment. Nick continues to chuckle every so often, amazed by my response to his touch.

"Oh, Daimon!"

Shit!

Nick freezes and my eyelids fly open. I yank his hand out of my skirt and smooth down my shirt, trying to ignore the piercing glare he's casting in my direction.

"I'm sorry. I got carried away."

"Who's Daimon?"

I push past him and head for the dining table. "Just someone I knew a long time ago. He's… dead. He died recently and he was just on my mind. It's very… sad."

He sits across the table from me and stares at my full glass of wine for a moment. "I'm sorry to hear that your friend died. That must be very difficult."

Very difficult? I guess that's one way to describe what it feels like to kill someone you love.

Love? Do I *love* Daimon?

Suddenly, I feel sick to my stomach. Nick pushes my glass of wine toward me and I shake my head, feeling both ashamed for screaming Daimon's name while Nick was touching me and relieved. Relieved that I've at least admitted my feelings for Daimon to myself.

"Drink something. It will help you loosen up," Nick insists, tapping his finger on the stem of the wine glass.

I don't know if it's the motion of the boat or the weight of this new realization, but there's no way I'll be able to eat or drink right now. And there's no way I can drink wine while I'm pregnant with the child of the man I love.

I love Daimon.

My eyes well up with tears and I stare at the wine glass so I don't have to see the expression on

Nick's face.

I love my father's murderer. The father of my child.

My protector and my enemy.

I wipe the tears from my cheeks and look up into Nick's eyes. "I'm sorry. I just got a little emotional. I didn't mean for this to be awkward."

"No, it's okay. I understand. You lost someone very important, yes?"

I swallow the knot in my throat, then I sit up straight and draw in a long breath. "He was nobody. He… he's the person who burned me. And I swore I'd never let it happen again, so let's eat."

I'm pregnant. I'm allowed a brief emotional breakdown every now and then. Whether or not I love Daimon doesn't matter. If he *is* still alive, and he has the gall to show his face, I will finish him.

We get through the appetizer and soup course without any more tears or mishaps, but I've been guzzling so much water, I need a restroom quickly. I thought the weak bladder portion of a pregnancy came further down the road. At least, that's what I've seen on TV. What kind of person gets their sex education from the television? That would be me.

Placing my napkin next to my plate, I rise from the table, feeling a bit wobbly. "I'm fine," I say as Nick begins to rise. "I just have to use the restroom. I'll be right back."

The three men in tuxedos standing against the railing watch in confusion as I walk past them toward the back of the sailboat. One of them says something to me in Spanish as he follows me, but I just ignore him. I have to pee. I don't have time for translations.

Once I reach the stairs leading down into the cabin of the boat, the guy grabs my arm roughly.

"Don't touch me!" I shout, my instincts kicking in.

I twist his arm behind his back and slam him up against the wall of windows outside the staircase. His eyes widen with terror as I throw all my weight against his spine.

I sniff the air and quickly release him. "What's

that smell?"

I turn toward the cabin and both waiters grab my arms as I attempt to step inside.

"You are not allowed in there. Employees only," says the one I just pinned a few seconds ago.

"I have to use the restroom," I insist, though their grip continues to tighten around my arms. "*Baño.* I need to go."

The other waiter shakes his head. "You wait until we get back."

"I'll piss my pants if I have to wait that long!"

"You wait," he grunts.

Nick finally arrives. "*Qué están haciendo? Suelta la!*"

The men release me on Nick's orders and I rub my arms, pretending to be frightened. Taking a few deep breaths, I draw in that familiar scent of soap and oak. I'm losing my mind or these guys are hiding something down there. But I'm not getting past them unless I'm in the mood to maim or kill someone tonight. They're lucky I'm not.

"We need to go back," I say, turning into Nick

and wrapping my arms around his waist so he can protect me from the mean men. "I have to use the restroom and they won't let me go down there."

Nick argues with the men for a few more minutes, but they just block the entrance to the cabin and shake their heads, unwilling to budge. Finally, the boat is turned around and we arrive at the harbor twenty minutes later. Nick exchanges a few parting words with the men in tuxedos, whose faces remain hard and impassive. They look more like thugs than waiters now.

"I'm so sorry about that. I did not think they would do something like that. Are you sure you're okay?"

I chuckle as he continues to rub my arm as we walk home. "I'm fine. I promise." We climb the steps up to the street level and I try not to show my unease when I see the lights on inside my house. "Why don't you go ahead to your house. I'm just going to use the restroom at home and turn off the lights. I must have left those on."

He glances at my windows. "I don't remember

you leaving the lights on."

"Alyssa! Nicolas! I'm so happy to see you."

Nick and I turn toward the voice of my neighbor Elena. She's waving at us as she rushes down her steps and out onto the street to greet us.

"Elena, how are you?"

She smiles at me and tilts her head. "You look different. Your face is… puffy."

"Puffy?"

Did she just call me fat?

She shakes her head and turns to Nick. "Nicolas, *tienes un sacacorchos me puedes prestar?"* She turns to me and smiles. "A corkscrew. My husband lost ours again."

"Yes, come with me." Nick turns to me. "I'll wait for you at the house."

I nod as he sets off toward his cottage with Elena. As soon as they're inside, I turn toward my house and all the tiny hairs on my arms stand on end at the sight of the flickering light within. No, I didn't leave the lights on. And I especially didn't leave any candles on considering I don't own any candles.

I walk deliberately toward the front door, each step feeling heavier than the last. Placing my hand on the doorknob, I take a deep breath and let it out slowly. Then I turn the knob and push the door open.

My heart pounds against my ribs, pulses in my fingertips, and roars inside my ears. The entire living room, every surface, is covered in burning candles and freesia.

Each step I take, the smell becomes stronger, until I'm practically choking on it. The candle flames flicker, washing the petals of the flowers in dancing light.

The sight is mesmerizing.

The smell is overwhelming.

Then comes the sound as the door clicks behind me.

He's here.

"Ready to play, *chérie*?"

This story continues in *Unmasked* (Volume 3)

To find out how to purchase *Unmasked #3* go to:

cassialeo.com/unmasked

TURN THE PAGE

to read a preview of *KNOX (Volume 1)*

1

"Oh, Marco, don't stop."

His blue eyes are fixed on mine as he grinds into me, penetrating me deeper with each thrust. He's smiling at me. Oh, how I love that smile. I close my eyes and imagine the first time I saw that smile. Sitting in a booth in the corner of the shop. My father's arm around his shoulders, congratulating him.

"I've missed you, Marco."

I slide my hand behind his neck and pull his mouth against mine. It feels just like our first kiss, only better. We're older now. Wiser. I work for the department and Marco, he….

What does Marco do for a living?

"I love you, Marco. Tell me you love me."

He smiles as he kisses the corner of my mouth, but he doesn't say anything. I rake my fingers over his back and he doesn't make a sound. Not a hiss of air through his teeth or a soft moan. Nothing.

"Marco, please."

His cock is so thick, stretching me as he lifts my leg and pierces me slowly. I wrap my other leg around his hip, beckoning him further inside. Gasping, I throw my head back and he kisses the hollow of my throat. Ecstasy. This is pure, ethereal ecstasy. Dream-like. He slides his hand between us to caress my clit and my body quakes beneath him.

"I'm going to come, Marco. I'm coming! I'm coming!"

A soft chuckle wakes me and I find August next to me. The room is dark and I'm holding his hand prisoner between my thighs. A searing heat creeps up my cheeks as I realize I was dreaming about Marco again.

"Did you come?" August says, and I can hear the smug grin in his voice.

I push his hand back then turn around to face away from him. "Sorry."

He slides his arm around my waist and presses his chest against my back. "Goodnight, Becky."

2

"When was the last time you two went on a date?" Lita asks as we cross Vanderbilt.

A jerk in a silver hatchback blares his horn at us. Aren't hatchback drivers supposed to be stereotypically nice?

Lita and I pause on the corner of 42nd and Vanderbilt, Grand Central Terminal. I make a move to hug her goodbye and she laughs.

"Nuh-uh. Answer my question, Becky. When was the last time you and August went on a date?"

Her light-brown hair is a bit frizzy and her top lip is sweating from the sticky night air. She still manages to look gorgeous, like she just stepped off a photo shoot at an exotic location. Like she's been spritzed and primped to look exactly this way. Lita hates when people tell her she looks like a model. She actually thinks it's an insult. She desperately wants to be taken seriously. She gets this from working on Wall Street where her model stature and smooth voice must command notice.

"We're not dating. We're in a relationship. Date nights are for married couples trying to revive their relationship. There's nothing wrong with August and me. We're solid."

"Solid as the wall between you. When was the last time you went to his apartment?"

I want to launch into my usual spiel, but I'm actually afraid of how many times I've said the words aloud.

August and I have a comfortable relationship. We don't need to cling to each other every second of every day to feel secure. August loves me. I know that because he remembers my birthday and my favorite ice cream flavor. He knows how many kids I want (two, he wants four). And the biggest plus of all: he's not afraid to talk about marriage. He loves that I want a big wedding. And as soon as his blog is established enough that he can take more time off, we're getting married.

This is the part where you begin wondering if I'm actually this naïve. I'm not. I'm far from naïve. I may be a midtown girl now, but I was born and raised in Bensonhurst.

Born and raised in Bensonhurst. Whenever someone hears this phrase, they automatically assume I must be related to a crime family. Some people are brazen enough to come right out and ask me – in a joking manner, as if that makes the question less inappropriate. I just chuckle and say something like, "Wouldn't that be cool if I was?" That's what people want to hear.

People don't want to know the truth. They don't want to know that I left my entire family behind at the age of eighteen, except for the occasional phone call to my mother. They don't want to know that I chose a job in law enforcement with the hopes of sending my family a message. That message: I want nothing more to do with them. They especially don't want to know the things I've seen. Because people who idolize the mafia actually think that being the daughter of a crime boss is glamorous.

They imagine me in my fur coat, diamond encrusted fingernails. Maybe I'm dangling a designer handbag from my arm, stuffed with an adorable teacup Chihuahua. They imagine men who aren't afraid to get their hands bloody, coming home and using those same hands to rip off my lacy panties and claim me. They imagine a sexy, sinful cocktail of glamor spiked with a large dose of unyielding power.

For the most part, they're right. But they still haven't seen what I've seen. And what I saw in my living room, at the tender age of thirteen, was my father strangling a man I had come to know as Uncle Frank. A crime for which he was never punished, despite the many times my father has been in and out of jail for pettier crimes. The truth is that I barely know my father. I hope that never changes.

I look into Lita's wide gray eyes and I lie. "I was at August's apartment last week." I clap her arm awkwardly. She shakes her head so I lean in to hug her goodbye. "Enjoy your trip to Poughkeepsie. I'm sure your mom will have plenty of potato salad and honey-glazed ham to fatten you up."

"Don't rub it in."

She releases me and her fingers glance over my forearm as she walks away. As I watch her set off toward Grand Central Terminal, all I can think is that I *am* naïve. I am *so* naïve. I haven't been to August's apartment in four months.

I spin around to face the street and flag down the first cab. I'm going to August's apartment. I'm going to demand to know what is wrong with us. I'm twenty-three years old with a gorgeous twenty-five-year-old boyfriend who never takes me to his apartment. I know what he's going to say. He's going to say it's because I prefer midtown to the lower east side. Avoiding his apartment is just his way of trying to be agreeable. I'm not falling for that.

I throw my arm out angrily, determined to hail a cab and fly to August's apartment on a wind of fury. But the first car that stops for me is not a taxi. It's a shiny black SUV. And before I can step aside to try to hail a real cab, a man appears at my side, his fingers discreetly curling around my wrist.

"Your car is here." His dark eyes are locked on mine, never blinking, not even as the SUV door is flung open. "Your father needs to speak to you."

That's all he has to say.

3

I climb into the SUV and I'm not surprised to find that there's another man in there waiting to receive me. Both he and the guy who met me on the curb are wearing dark suits and sunglasses. I'm sure if I could see anything inside this dark SUV, I'd find earpieces shining inside their ears.

When all three of us are settled into the backseat, the SUV pulls away from Grand Central Terminal and sets off down 42nd. The bigger guy on my left reaches behind his back and my heart stops. They wouldn't kill me just like that, would they? I brace myself for whatever he's about to retrieve from behind his back, my body tensed and ready to flail about. But when he pulls his hand out, he's holding a large piece of black cloth. Upon further inspection, I notice it's a black hood.

I can't see his eyes through the sunglasses, but the fact that he's offering it to me instead of putting it on me himself seems to be some show of respect. They're not going to kill me. They don't even want to hurt me. They're too afraid of my father. Which means that my father is not as angry with me for abandoning the family as I had imagined. Or … he wants something.

I huff as I snatch the black silk hood out of his hand. I quickly note my surroundings before I pull it over my head. We're just approaching Fifth Avenue. Everything goes black and I try to keep track of the many turns the vehicle makes. But it doesn't take long for me to realize that they're probably taking me on a winding route just to confuse me.

When the car finally stops and the engine dies, my stomach vaults. I haven't seen my father in four years since the last time I visited Mom at home and he was actually home – a rare occasion. I was nineteen and terribly homesick during Spring Break at Hunter College where I was studying, of all things, creative writing. My visit home was supposed to be soothing and relaxing and familiar. Instead, my father decided to get out of jail three weeks early and I left the house without him uttering a word to me; his eyes watching me as I walked out the door, his lips unable to break a smile or silence for his only child.

The worst part about leaving home is the conversations with my mother. She's had to endure my father's grief over the fact that she never gave him more than one child. She's never admitted it, but I can imagine him calling her useless. My mother is far from useless. Without my mother, I'd probably be traipsing around town with diamond-encrusted fingernails and a designer dog. My mother taught me to want more.

But I must admit that, as they help me out of the SUV and my heart pounds so hard I can barely breathe, it's not just fear of my father that has me this stressed. I'm also intrigued. For my father to have me essentially kidnapped and forced to meet with him, he must be desperate.

My summer sandals crunch on the gravelly pavement as someone grips my forearm and guides me forward. A door creaks open and I'm blasted with a cool gust of air-conditioned air. The smell of rubber and grease stings the inside of my nostrils as I'm pulled farther inside this new environment.

The whoosh of another door opening.

More walking.

Stop.

Is he here?

Silence.

"Brace yourself, kid." This warning issued by the guy on my right feels more ominous than it should. It's just my father in there, isn't it?

The silk hood is slipped off my head and we're standing in the middle of a wide garage with hydraulic lifts and tires and an assortment of equipment for repairing cars. But there are no cars in this garage. One person stands about ten feet away from me, facing me.

And it's not my father.

Other books by Cassia Leo

EROTIC ROMANCE

KNOX Series

LUKE Series

CHASE Series

CONTEMPORARY ROMANCE

Forever Ours (Shattered Hearts #0.5)

Relentless (Shattered Hearts #1)

Pieces of You (Shattered Hearts #2)

Bring Me Home (Shattered Hearts #3)

Abandon (Shattered Hearts #3.5)

Black Box (stand-alone novel)

PARANORMAL ROMANCE

Parallel Spirits (Carrier Spirits #1)

About the Author

New York Times and *USA Today* bestselling author Cassia Leo loves her coffee, chocolate, and margaritas with salt. When she's not writing, she spends way too much time watching old reruns of *Friends* and *Sex and the City*. When she's not watching reruns, she's usually enjoying the California sunshine or reading – sometimes both.

Made in the USA
Lexington, KY
28 June 2014